Why did she have to open her big mouth?

"Jessica! It's almost eight thirty!" Lila cried, shutting off the music. Everyone on the dance floor stopped moving and looked around, as if they were expecting an earthquake any second.

Jessica chewed her thumbnail and studied her watch. One minute until my life is over. *She watched the second hand sweep around the dial. Each second seemed to last forever.*

"Five . . . four . . . three . . . two . . . one!" *the crowd shouted.*

They all stood waiting in silence.

Nothing happened.

"Well?" *Lila said, coming over to her.* "Where's the earthquake?"

"Uh . . ." *Jessica faltered as she noticed a hundred faces, practically everyone at Sweet Valley Middle School, looking at her from all over the room.* Dynamite, *she thought miserably.* I should have exploded some dynamite outside the house.

She would have gone to jail, but it would probably be better than having to walk into school tomorrow morning and face everyone.

SWEET VALLEY TWINS
AND FRIENDS

Jessica and the Earthquake

Written by
Jamie Suzanne

Created by
FRANCINE PASCAL

BANTAM BOOKS
NEW YORK · TORONTO · LONDON · SYDNEY · AUCKLAND

To Zachary Logan Stein

RL 4, 008-012

JESSICA AND THE EARTHQUAKE
A Bantam Book / January 1994

*Sweet Valley High® and Sweet Valley Twins and Friends® are
registered trademarks of Francine Pascal*

Conceived by Francine Pascal

*Produced by Daniel Weiss Associates, Inc.
33 West 17th Street
New York, NY 10011*

Cover art by James Mathewuse

ISBN: 0-553-48061-8

Published simultaneously in the United States and Canada

*Bantam Books are published by Bantam Books, a division of Bantam
Doubleday Dell Publishing Group, Inc. Its trademark, consisting of the
words "Bantam Books" and the portrayal of a rooster, is Registered in
U.S. Patent and Trademark Office and in other countries. Marca
Registrada. Bantam Books, 1540 Broadway, New York, New York 10036.*

PRINTED IN THE UNITED STATES OF AMERICA

OPM   0 9 8 7 6 5 4 3

One

◇

Jessica Wakefield opened her eyes. There was a loud rattling noise coming from the bookshelf above her head. For a second she thought there must be a mouse up there, and she pulled the covers over her head. Then she heard the lamp on her bedside table shake too. *What's going on?* she wondered, sitting up.

She rubbed her eyes and looked at her alarm clock. It said 3:42 in the morning. What in the world was she doing *awake* at 3:42? She didn't have to be up until seven.

Suddenly the rattling stopped. It was probably just a garbage truck making the house shake, she decided, snuggling back under the covers. They were always out in the middle of the night.

She yawned, curled up into a ball, and fell back asleep.

*   *   *

"Come on, Dad," Elizabeth Wakefield said, pouring some toasted cornflakes into her bowl. "You're kind of early for April Fools'."

"I'm not kidding. Just wait a second—I'm sure they'll repeat it on the seven o'clock news report," Mr. Wakefield told her, shaking out the morning newspaper.

"Repeat what?" Jessica stood in the doorway, rubbing her eyes.

"Nice circles under your eyes. Did you draw those yourself?" Steven, Jessica and Elizabeth's fourteen-year-old brother, asked.

Jessica glared at him and sat beside Elizabeth, her twin sister, at the breakfast table.

Elizabeth passed her the orange juice. "Did you stay up late studying for the science quiz?"

"Jessica? Stay up late to *study*?" Steven teased. "She was probably doing her nails—"

"Shh," Mr. Wakefield instructed as the brief jingle that introduced the seven o'clock news played on the small kitchen radio.

"Today's top story is a shaky one," the radio announcer began. "This morning, at approximately three forty, an earthquake occurred right here in Sweet Valley. It wasn't a big one, but it did register three point two on the Richter scale. Scientists say they're baffled by the unexpected quake. Sweet

Valley hasn't witnessed an earthquake since 1972. Experts are currently investigating the possibility of aftershocks. In a related story—"

"I can't believe it!" Elizabeth cried. "An earthquake hit town for the first time in over twenty years, and I slept right through it!"

"Me too," Steven grumbled. "Finally we get an earthquake, and we don't get a day off from school or anything."

"Are you saying you wanted the quake to be bigger?" asked Mr. Wakefield.

"Sure. It would have been cool," Steven said.

"Not if lots of people had been hurt, and our house had been damaged," Mrs. Wakefield said. "Earthquakes can be very, very dangerous."

Elizabeth shook her head. "Three forty in the morning. You'd think *one* of us would have woken up."

Jessica was dumping Corny-O's into her bowl when she suddenly looked up. "Wait a second!" she cried. "It wasn't three forty, it was three forty-two!" The cereal poured over the top of her bowl onto the table.

"Jess!" her mother yelled, grabbing the box before cereal flowed onto the floor.

"Sorry," Jessica said. "I just remembered that I woke up last night, right when the earthquake happened! I was so sleepy I forgot at first. But I woke up at *exactly* three forty-two."

"That's really weird," Elizabeth said.

Steven shook his head. "Jess, you wouldn't wake up if a plane landed in your bedroom."

"I did so wake up!" Jessica insisted. "Everything was shaking in my room. I just figured it was a garbage truck or something. I didn't realize it was an *earthquake*."

"You must be really sensitive to the vibrations or something," Elizabeth said.

"Maybe we need an earthquake alarm to add to our smoke alarm," Mrs. Wakefield mused.

"Who needs an earthquake alarm when you have me?" Jessica said happily. "I would have woken you guys up if it was serious."

"We don't need an alarm for earthquakes—we need one for idiots," Steven said to Jessica.

Jessica stuck out her tongue. "You're just jealous you missed it."

"Look, Elizabeth!" Jessica pointed at a crack in the sidewalk as she and Elizabeth were walking to school together that morning.

"What about it?" Elizabeth asked. A few small flowers poked through the inch-wide crack in the concrete.

"That must be from the earthquake!" Jessica said. Her blue-green eyes sparkled with excitement.

Elizabeth gave her a suspicious look. "Jessica, I

don't think so," she said. "For one thing, those flowers couldn't have grown since last night. And for another, the sidewalk is full of cracks that have been here forever. You just haven't noticed them before."

"Well, maybe not. But I *did* notice the earthquake last night. Can you believe I'm the only one who even woke up for it? You know what that means, don't you?" Jessica asked.

"What?" Elizabeth asked.

"I can predict earthquakes," Jessica said. "Remember how I told you I felt funny before I went to bed?"

"That was because you ate a humongous slice of chocolate cake with two scoops of banana ice cream on top," Elizabeth said, tightening the blue polkadot scrunchy around her long blond ponytail. "You told me you had a stomachache."

"No, I told you I felt *weird*," Jessica said. "Now I know why—the earthquake was coming!"

Elizabeth shook her head. It wasn't the first time that Jessica had let her imagination run away with her. She was always getting crazy ideas. For a while she had actually been convinced she and Elizabeth were psychic.

Sometimes Elizabeth felt as though her twin had been dropped off from another planet. She and Jessica were best friends, and they looked identical in every way, from their long sun-streaked blond hair and blue-green eyes to their matching dimples.

But on the inside they couldn't have been more different.

Jessica belonged to a club at school called the Unicorns. The Unicorns considered themselves the most popular girls at Sweet Valley Middle School, and spent most of their time gossiping, or talking about boys and clothes. In Elizabeth's opinion, some of the girls in the club, like Lila Fowler and Janet Howell, were total snobs. She had been invited to join the club at the beginning of the school year, but had decided not to.

Elizabeth tended to be more quiet, though she was popular too. She loved horseback riding, reading mysteries, and hanging out with her close friends, Amy Sutton and Maria Slater. She wanted to be a writer when she grew up and spent a lot of time working on articles for the *Sweet Valley Sixers*, the middle school's weekly newspaper.

"Listen, Jess, it's awesome that you felt the earthquake," Elizabeth said. "But I don't think it means anything special. When we get to school, I bet we'll find out you're not the only one who woke up for the earthquake."

"Not for," Jessica said. "*Before* it happened."

"We'll see," Elizabeth said.

Meanwhile Steven was waiting at home for Cathy Connors, his girlfriend, to meet him at his house so they could ride their bicycles to Sweet Valley High together. He was watching music videos on television as he did some last-minute reviewing for a history test.

"Coming up next, the world-premiere video of the Katybugs' new video, 'Does This Make Sense?'" he heard the veejay announce.

Steven leaned forward on the couch. The Katybugs were one of his favorite groups, if not *the* favorite. Just at that moment there was a knock on the kitchen door. "Come on in!" he yelled.

"Hey, Steven," Cathy said. "Ready to go?"

"Just a sec," Steven said. "Check this out—it's the new video from the Katybugs." He made room for her on the couch.

The video opened with a shot of a field of cattle, then the camera zoomed in on one cow. Then one of the band members was standing beside it, and a diagram was superimposed on the cow. The lead singer started pointing out different sections of the animal. "Prime rib, filet mignon, shank," he sang. "Delmonico, T-bone, flank."

"What is this?" Cathy asked.

"Shh," Steven said.

The video went on, and the band switched to different animals as they sang the lyrics, "Does this make sense to *you*?" Along the bottom of the screen, printed lines appeared explaining how the different animals were treated as they were being raised for food.

"Can you believe that?" Steven shook his head. "They actually cut off chickens' beaks."

"Pretty gross," Cathy agreed, making a face.

Steven watched as the lead singer walked into a pigsty and petted a large hog. "That's so sad!" Steven exclaimed. "Pigs have to stay in those tiny, dark stalls for almost their entire lives!"

"That is really sad," Cathy agreed.

The video ended with the four band members standing in the middle of a chicken coop with thousands of chickens in tiny boxes.

"What a cool song," Steven said when it was over. "It really makes you think."

"Yeah, it does," Cathy said. "I never knew the Katybugs were such a serious band."

"I guess it's a pretty serious issue," Steven said. He jotted down a note on his notebook: Buy New Katybugs CD After School.

"I learned a bunch about the way animals are treated in biology class last month," Cathy said. "I never realized what it was like, what a huge business it is. Some of it's unbelievable."

Steven sighed. "I don't think I'll ever look at a hamburger in the same way again."

Cathy laughed. "You don't *look* at them anyway, Steven. You just inhale them. Come on, let's go. We're going to be late."

Steven just sat on the couch for another minute, staring at the television. He couldn't get over everything he'd just seen. "Seriously, Cath. The thought of eating meat right now makes me feel sick."

"You'll get over it," Cathy said, hoisting her backpack over her shoulder. "Besides, if you didn't eat burgers you'd probably starve to death."

"I don't eat them *that* much," Steven said defensively.

"I call twice a day *that* much," Cathy teased. "At least one hamburger for lunch, and you go to Hughie's Burger Shack almost every day after basketball practice."

"Not every day."

Cathy shrugged. "Look, Steven, becoming a vegetarian is a cool thing to do. I just don't think you could do it. It's a whole different way of life."

"I could so do it," Steven said indignantly.

Cathy looked at him skeptically. "If you say so."

Two

"It's unbelievable—neither one of us woke up during the earthquake," Elizabeth said to Amy on the steps in front of school. "We're supposed to be news reporters, and we slept right through a major story."

"Well, my mom didn't notice it either, if that's any consolation," Amy said. Mrs. Sutton was a news reporter for the local television station.

"Yeah, but Jessica did, and *she's* the heaviest sleeper in the whole family." Elizabeth laughed. "Now she thinks she's got some kind of special powers."

"I bet lots of other people woke up too," Amy said. "Hey, I've got an idea. Why don't we write a *Sixers* article about how students dealt with the quake?"

"That's a great idea," Elizabeth agreed. "We can

do profiles of different people's reactions to it. Come on, let's get started."

They walked over to where Ken Matthews, Aaron Dallas, and Todd Wilkins were standing.

"Hi," Todd greeted them. "What's up?"

"We were just talking about the earthquake this morning," Elizabeth said. "What were you doing when it happened?"

"Dreaming about playing in the NBA," Todd said. "I slept right through it."

"Me too," Ken said. "I didn't wake up until seven, when my alarm clock went off. No one else in my family woke up either."

"How about you, Aaron?" Amy asked.

Aaron shook his head. "I didn't wake up until my mom started shaking me. I stayed up late watching a horror movie and I was totally zonked."

"Really?" Elizabeth couldn't believe it. Had everyone except Jessica slept through the earthquake? "Look, there's Winston," she said. "Let's ask him."

"Hey, Winston." Amy motioned him over. "What did you think about the earthquake this morning?"

Winston gave her a puzzled look. "What earthquake?"

"You haven't even heard about it?" Amy asked him.

"Oh, you mean when the ground was shaking last night? I thought that was Mrs. Arnette jogging past my house," Winston said, laughing. "I was afraid she was coming over to make me take a retest on famous Civil War battles."

Elizabeth laughed. "I guess you didn't wake up."

Winston shook his head. "I always make a point of sleeping through natural disasters."

Amy and Elizabeth moved on to interview other students. They talked to about fifteen more people before the bell rang, signaling the beginning of homeroom.

"It's amazing. *Everybody* slept through the earthquake," Amy said, stopping in front of her homeroom.

"This is going to be a very short profile," Elizabeth commented.

"Maybe Jessica's right—maybe she does have some kind of special sensitivity," Amy said.

Elizabeth shook her head. "I'm not falling for that one again. We'll find *someone* else who woke up last night."

"So then, all the books on my bookshelf started shaking. One fell off the end, right into the trash can!" Jessica said.

"You're kidding," Ellen Riteman said. "Which book was it?"

Jessica rolled her eyes. "Who cares what book it was, Ellen? Anyway, there was so much going on, I didn't have time to look."

"So what else happened?" Danny Jackson asked.

"Yeah, did anything break?" Aaron asked.

"Well, I have a framed collage of photos on the wall, and the glass was shaking, like it was about to break," Jessica said. "I was just getting out of bed to take it off the wall when a heavy glass unicorn I have skidded off my bookshelf. I had to make a leaping catch or it would have shattered on the floor!"

Jessica glanced at Lila, who wasn't saying anything. Typical Lila. She wasn't even excited by the fact that her best friend had witnessed a major earthquake. OK, so maybe it wasn't major, but it was exciting.

"Jessica, would you mind holding off on your dramatic stories until after class?" Mr. Seigel, the science teacher, asked in an irritated voice.

"Don't you think it would be interesting to talk about the earthquake today?" Jessica asked. "They're so . . . y'know . . . scientific."

"We covered earthquakes last month," Mr. Seigel said. "Now, everyone, take your seats and let's get started. We have a lot to do today." He placed a sheet of paper on Jessica's desk. "Including a pop quiz on the earthworm."

"Nice try," Lila whispered to Jessica.

Steven knocked on his science teacher's door. "Excuse me, Mr. Wheaton, are you busy?" he asked.

"Just getting some notes together for today's class," Mr. Wheaton said. "Come on in."

Steven walked into his office and sat down. He shifted nervously in his chair. Science wasn't exactly his best subject. Usually when he came to Mr. Wheaton's office it was to talk about a test he'd bombed.

"So what can I help you with?" Mr. Wheaton asked.

"Well, I saw a music video this morning," Steven said.

Mr. Wheaton raised one eyebrow. "Really."

Steven cleared his throat. "And it was all about things that are done to animals when they're being raised for food."

"Uh-huh," Mr. Wheaton said. "And what did you want to know?"

"I guess, uh, whether it was all true or not," Steven said. "I was kind of hoping some of the stuff was exaggerated."

"So basically what you're talking about is research." Mr. Wheaton nodded. "What any good scientist needs to know—the facts. Well, let me see here." He ran his finger along the bookshelves beside his desk. "Aha." He pulled a book out and handed it to Steven. "This should help."

Steven looked at the heavy textbook. It was called *Animals: Friends and Food*.

"And how about these?" Mr. Wheaton grabbed several brochures and piled them on top of the book in Steven's hands. "Now, if you'll excuse me, I need to get my notes together for my lecture."

"Thanks," Steven said, juggling all the brochures on his way out the door.

"You're welcome," Mr. Wheaton said. "By the way, if you're interested in getting some extra credit, you might write a paper putting together all that information."

Steven stood in the hallway outside the office. "A paper? Um, yeah. Maybe. Good idea." He was starting to feel a little queasy again. He glanced at the top brochure on the pile. It was called "Bacon and Bacteria."

If I read this pile of stuff, I really may never eat meat again.

"So you're proposing a feature article about the earthquake, yet you didn't actually experience it firsthand?" Mr. Bowman, Elizabeth's English teacher, asked her after class.

Elizabeth shook her head. "Nope."

"Neither did I," said Amy. "And neither did practically anyone else."

"Well, I don't know," Mr. Bowman said, straightening his loud purple and green tie. He served as the adviser to the *Sixers,* and approved ideas for articles.

"But that shouldn't matter," Elizabeth said. "I mean, people write about stuff they haven't actually witnessed all the time."

"True." Mr. Bowman smiled. "I just think that a *real* journalist would have woken up during an earthquake," he said in a teasing voice.

Elizabeth looked at Amy and frowned. "I know. It would be a lot easier to write if we'd experienced it ourselves."

"And probably more exciting," Mr. Bowman said.

"Well, what if there's another earthquake soon? You know, an aftershock or something," Amy said. "I heard on the news it's common to get a series of quakes in a row. Could we write an article then?"

"Sure. I think an earthquake would make a great feature," Mr. Bowman said. "If you're awake for it."

"Oh, we will be," Elizabeth said. "I'm not missing the next quake, no matter what."

"Are you serious, Jessica? Your glass unicorn broke? That's terrible!" Kimberly Haver said in the hallway after English class.

"Yeah, I know. I tried to catch it, but I was too busy making sure my photo collage didn't fall on the floor. It just . . . shattered." Jessica tried to look upset. "Glass everywhere."

"But if you woke up before the earthquake, how come you couldn't save your stuff?" Grace Oliver asked.

"I have a pretty big room," Jessica said. "I couldn't be everywhere at once." The truth was she had just lain in bed during the whole thing, but no one else needed to know that. No one else had even blinked during the earthquake. They'd believe anything she told them.

"It's so weird, how no one woke up except you," Grace said.

"Well, I've been thinking about it a lot, and I was wondering if maybe I'm really sensitive to earthquakes and natural disasters," Jessica said. "I saw a TV talk show once where they were interviewing people who had predicted tornadoes and hurricanes. Only no one would listen to them."

"So what happened?" Tamara Chase asked.

"People got hurt, lots of houses were destroyed. Nobody was prepared," Jessica said smugly. "You know, some people have special scientific senses. It's really incredible."

"So do you think you do?" Kimberly asked, looking at Jessica admiringly.

"I might," Jessica said. "You never know."

"Hey, Jessica!" Peter Jeffries called to her as she and Lila hurried down the hall toward gym class. "I heard you were awake for the earthquake."

"Was I ever," Jessica said. "It was unbelievable."

Lila sighed loudly. "Here we go again," she muttered.

"So what happened?" Peter asked.

"Well." Jessica tossed her hair over her shoulder. "Last night before I went to bed, I felt incredibly strange. Like something was going to happen that I shouldn't miss. When I was falling asleep, I actually had an image of a really loud rumble, and then my whole house crumbling to the ground."

"That's really weird," Peter said.

The only thing rumbling was my stomach, Jessica thought, glancing at Lila beside her. But what harm was there in making the story a little more exciting? It wasn't as if anyone could disprove it. "Yeah. Anyway, I finally fell asleep, and then all of a sudden, at three forty-two in the morning, I jumped up in bed. A few seconds later, everything in my room started shaking."

"What was it like?" Peter asked. "Did stuff break?"

Jessica shook her head and tried to look serious. "It was so scary. The shaking got stronger, and stronger, and then my pictures and books started shaking off the walls—"

"You're kidding," Peter said. "Wow."

Lila sighed again, sounding completely exasperated. "Come *on*, Jessica, let's go."

"No, I'm totally serious," Jessica told Peter, ignoring Lila. "A glass unicorn I have smashed on the floor, and my mirror fell off the wall—"

"Uh-oh. That means seven years' bad luck," Peter said.

"I know," Jessica said. "But the scariest thing is, there was a crack in the wall that started getting wider and wider. I thought the house was going to fall apart!"

"Sounds like you were really lucky," Peter said, shaking his head. "The quake must have happened right under your house. Nobody else in your family woke up?"

"No," Jessica said. "You know what? I think maybe that's because it was right under my *bedroom*."

"That could be," Peter said, nodding. "That's really intense, Jessica."

"Give me a break," Lila mumbled.

Three

"Is that all you're going to eat?" Steven's best friend, Joe Howell, asked, staring down at Steven's tray on Monday in the cafeteria of Sweet Valley High.

Steven glanced down at his tray. On it were a bowl of butterscotch pudding, a brownie, and a salad. "Yeah, why?"

"Because you usually eat about twelve tacos when we have Mexican food," Joe said. "What's the deal—are you sick?"

"No," Steven said. For some reason he felt kind of embarrassed about telling Joe how he'd decided to change his diet. Joe would probably think it was stupid.

They sat down and Steven watched Joe take a huge bite of his beef taco. "I saw the Katybugs' new video before school," Steven said.

"Yeah? How was it?" Joe asked, sipping a glass of milk.

"Pretty cool," Steven said. "It's all about how cruel and wasteful it is to eat meat. Did you know it takes sixteen pounds of grain and soybeans to produce one pound of beef?"

"Fascinating," Joe said. He took another big bite.

"So anyway, I decided to give up red meat for a while," Steven said.

Joe started choking on his taco. "You? Not eat meat for a while?" he gasped. "That's like you deciding not to breathe air for a while."

Steven glared at him angrily. "What is this? You and Cathy act like I'm some kind of caveman. For your information, I haven't had any meat all day."

"Dude, it's only eleven thirty," Joe said.

Steven frowned. The smell of tacos drifted his way, and he felt his stomach churning. Then he thought about the little calf in the video again, and how cute and helpless it looked. "Yeah, well, you watch. I'm going to stick to this," Steven said firmly.

Joe nodded. "Right. Well, I guess I won't be seeing you at the Dairi *Burger* for a while, then, huh?" he asked.

"I can still go," Steven said. "I'll just have . . . fries, that's all."

"Sure you will," Joe said. "Sure."

*   *   *

"It was unbelievable how quiet it was, actually," Jessica told a group gathered around her in the lunchroom. "I mean, I'm not surprised I'm one of the only people who woke up."

"I thought you said there was a crash in your bedroom," Aaron said.

"Right," Jessica said. "Exactly. But it was just a . . . little crash. No one else in the house heard it."

"That's so cool you woke up for it," Bruce Patman told her. "I wish I had." Bruce was one of the best-looking and definitely one of the richest seventh-graders at school, and he wasn't easily impressed. Jessica was psyched that he was paying so much attention to her.

In fact, Jessica felt as though everyone looking at her was hanging on her every word. They were all fascinated by the earthquake. She felt sort of obligated to make it sound as exciting as possible.

"You know what I want to find out?" Jessica said. "I was wondering if maybe the—what's it called? The exact spot where the earthquake hits?"

"Epicenter," Mandy Miller said.

"Right," Jessica said, nodding. "I was thinking, maybe the epicenter was right under our house!"

Lila groaned. "Give it up already, will you, Jess? It was only one dumb earthquake. Besides, Daddy told me it only registered three point two on the Richter scale. That's nothing to get excited about."

"On the contrary." Lloyd Benson pushed his way closer to Jessica. "Actually, it's quite remarkable."

Jessica shot Lila a triumphant look. *So there.* Lloyd was Sweet Valley Middle School's official science nerd. Everyone called him "Lloyd Bunsen Burner." He had won the science fair every year since he was six, and if anyone knew anything about earthquakes, it was Lloyd. Lloyd was a pretty nice guy, Jessica thought. Of course, he talked like an encyclopedia, but he couldn't help that.

"Thank you, Lloyd," Jessica said. "So you didn't wake up during it either?"

"Not at all." Lloyd wheezed and pushed his heavy black-framed glasses up on his nose. "In fact, I am quite intrigued by your story."

"Really?" Jessica said, casting a nervous glance at Bruce and Aaron. She didn't want to talk to Lloyd *too* long. She didn't want it to seem as if they were really great friends or anything.

"Did you know that scientists have machines that try to do exactly what you did?" Lloyd asked. "They've been attempting to predict earthquakes for years. And here you are, only a sixth-grader—"

"Almost seventh," Jessica said, smiling at Bruce.

"And you had a feeling several hours before the quake, and then woke up right before it occurred."

Lloyd shook his head and his glasses slipped down a bit. "Truly amazing."

Jessica shrugged. "What can I say?"

Lila rolled her eyes.

"I bet they'd be very interested in hearing about you at the Center for Earthquake Research," Lloyd went on, adjusting the belt of his light-blue polyester pants.

"You really think so?" Jessica asked.

"Yeah, as a total fraud," she heard Lila whisper to Janet Howell.

"Yes, I do think so," Lloyd said. "And that's why I've decided to follow you around for the next week."

"Huh?" Jessica asked.

"That's right. I want to study you for my next science project," Lloyd explained, smiling at Jessica. "I'll be your shadow for the next week. Together we can determine whether there will be any more seismic activity. How does that sound?"

Like a nightmare! Jessica thought as Lila and the other Unicorns burst out laughing.

"It serves her right," Lila said to Janet when Jessica finally went to stand in the lunch line. "The way she's been bragging all day, she deserves to be followed around by Lloyd." The Unicorns were all sitting together in their special reserved table in the lunchroom, which they called the Unicorner.

Lila had heard at least three different versions of the earthquake from Jessica so far, and she was really getting sick of it. Of course, it was typical Jessica. Lila could think of at least a hundred other times when Jessica had exaggerated a story just to make herself look better.

"Yeah. But she deserves to be followed around for a month, not just a week," Janet agreed. "Talk about hogging the spotlight. She's acting like she's a genius or something."

"The funny thing is, you know what a heavy sleeper Jessica is," Mandy said.

Tamara nodded. "At our last sleepover we teased her hair into a beehive and she didn't even budge."

"Right," Lila said. "So *we* all know it's only luck that made her wake up when everyone else was asleep. She probably had a bad dream or something."

"And we know she couldn't predict an earthquake if her life depended on it," Janet said. "Did you hear her say she had special scientific senses?"

"Yeah, so does my golden retriever," Tamara said. "He knows when it's time for dinner every night."

Everyone laughed.

"OK, so what are we going to do about it?" Janet asked.

"Maybe by tomorrow she'll figure out that

everyone's bored with her story," Ellen said.

"Are you kidding? Jessica?" Lila shook her head. "No, we have to prove that she's lying somehow. I haven't figured out how yet, but I will."

"Shh. Here she comes," Mary Wallace warned.

Jessica set her tray on the table. "Look at these chocolate-chip cookies. They're all crumbled," she said. "I wonder if it has anything to do with the earthquake."

"It's called cafeteria food," Lila said, rolling her eyes. She'd had enough. There had to be some way to show everyone what a fake Jessica and her earthquake stories were, and she was going to find it.

Four

"You're giving up meat *and* going to the library, all in one day?" Cathy commented after school as she and Steven unlocked their mountain bikes. "Are you sure that earthquake didn't shake something loose in your brain?"

Steven laughed. "No, it's just that I want to check out some of the information that was in that video. Plus I want to look at all the junk Wheaton gave me."

Cathy gave him a puzzled look. "You're really interested in this, aren't you?"

"Sure," Steven said. "I mean, I respect that lead singer who writes all the Katybugs' songs. If he thinks this is important, then it is. I want to know all about it."

"I should have known the library trip had nothing to do with homework," Cathy teased. "Well, have fun. I'll see you later."

"See you," Steven called. He got on his bike and rode to the town library.

"Do you have a section on animal books?" Steven asked the librarian at the front desk.

"What kind of book do you want?" she asked. "Photographs? Biology? Animal psychology?"

"Um . . ." Steven drummed his fingers on the desk. "I guess one about how they're treated. How pigs and cows are raised for food and all that," he said, shifting his backpack to his other shoulder.

"Ah! Animal rights," the librarian said, nodding, and went to get a book for him.

Animal rights? Steven wondered after she was gone. *Is that what I'm doing? Sounds impressive.*

Jessica was walking home by herself from a Boosters practice that afternoon when she heard someone walking behind her. She slowed down for a second and heard heavy shoes on the concrete sidewalk slowing down too. She stopped, and whoever was following her stopped too.

Jessica whirled around, hoping to scare them off by surprising them. "Lloyd!" she yelled. "What do you think you're doing?"

Lloyd walked up to her. "I told you, I have to follow you around for my science project. I'm going to write a big paper about you and send it to the Center for Earthquake Research. We may even go there together and give a special presentation."

Jessica sighed in frustration. "Do you really have to follow me every second?"

"In order for it to be an accurate observation, yes," Lloyd said. He switched his little briefcase from one hand to the other.

"Well, I have to get home—my mom's waiting for me," Jessica said impatiently. "I have to help make dinner."

"OK, but I want to ask you a few questions first," Lloyd said.

Jessica sighed again. "Fine."

"Number one, you probably know that sometimes earthquakes occur in clusters. There's a very good chance there'll be another one within the next few days," Lloyd said.

Jessica didn't remember hearing that in science class, but if Lloyd said it, it had to be true. Half the time it seemed as though he knew more than Mr. Seigel. "And?" she asked.

"Well, do you sense anything yet?" Lloyd asked.

Only intense aggravation, Jessica thought. "No, I don't," she told Lloyd. "Actually, I'm fairly certain nothing's going to happen this afternoon." Jessica didn't want to lie, but she had to do something to get rid of Lloyd. What would Janet and Lila say if they saw her standing on the sidewalk, chatting with Lloyd? She'd never hear the end of it.

"I thought maybe we could watch the weather channel together this afternoon and see what they say about the possibility of another tremor," Lloyd went on, completely oblivious to the fact that Jessica was already walking away.

"No, I don't think so," Jessica said. "That would be cheating, wouldn't it? I mean, in order for the project to be a success, I have to feel the earthquake coming on my own, right?"

"Uh . . ." Lloyd hesitated.

"Great. So I'll see you tomorrow," Jessica said, hurrying away down the street.

Finally, she thought. If waking up during an earthquake meant she had to hang out with Lloyd Benson, she was beginning to wish she'd slept right through it like everybody else!

"You know what we have to do?" Elizabeth asked. "We have to stay up for the rest of this week. One of us has to be awake all the time so we can catch the next earthquake."

She and Amy were sitting at the table in the Wakefields' kitchen after school.

"We do?" Amy asked.

"Sure. You heard Mr. Bowman. He just about challenged us to do it," Elizabeth said. "We have to."

Amy sighed. "I guess. But what if there's not another earthquake? Or what if there is, but it's not for another two weeks? I mean, what are we supposed to do?"

"Chances are, if there is another one it will be soon. So let's try to stay up for the next three days. We can do that, can't we? It might be sort of fun. I'll ask my mom and dad if you can stay over." Elizabeth looked up and saw Jessica appear in the doorway. "Hi, Jess," she said.

"Hi," Jessica said. "You won't believe who followed me home." She opened the refrigerator and took out a carton of orange juice. "Lloyd Benson. He has this crazy idea that I'm going to be his next science project, just because I'm extra sensitive to earthquakes."

Amy started laughing. "More like extra *lucky*," she said.

"It wasn't luck," Jessica insisted. She sat down at the kitchen table across from Elizabeth. "Anyway, what are you guys doing?"

"Writing an article about the quake," Elizabeth said. "We got some books from the school library to use for research."

Jessica picked up one of the books and started leafing through it. "Hey, this is pretty cool," she said a few minutes later. "It says that plates under the earth move all the time. Los Angeles is actually moving toward San Francisco at the rate of about two inches per year. Wow. So Lloyd was right—another earthquake *could* happen soon."

Amy looked at Elizabeth and raised her eyebrows. "Of course, you probably know when the next earthquake will be, with your special sensitivity and all—right, Jessica?" Amy teased.

"Yeah, since you predicted the last one," Elizabeth said, trying to suppress a smile. "Maybe you could help us. We want to make sure we're there for the next one. Can you tell when it'll happen?"

"I might," Jessica said in a serious tone. "Let me see if I feel anything." She closed her eyes and put her hands on the table. "Hmm . . ."

"Jessica, it's not a séance," Elizabeth said, laughing.

"Shh! I'm waiting for vibrations," Jessica said. Her forehead wrinkled and she seemed to be concentrating. A minute later she said, "Hmm. Nothing yet, but maybe it's too early."

Amy laughed. "Jessica, you tried to make us believe you were psychic before, remember?"

"Yeah, well I was—I mean I am. Sort of," Jessica said defensively. "And anyway, I told you I felt funny before I went to bed last night, didn't I? You can't deny that. And I am the only one at school who even budged during it. Not even Lloyd Bunsen Burner, Mr. Science Fair, woke up—*that* should tell you something."

"Yeah, that he was tired," Amy said.

"Whatever," Elizabeth said, shaking her head. Trust Jessica to let a night of indigestion turn into some special power of hers. "Maybe you should read some more of these books," she told her sister. "Maybe there are other stories of people with special earthquake-predicting powers."

"Actually, it does say something in this book about sensing earthquakes," Amy said.

"Really?" Jessica asked excitedly.

"Yeah. It says that dogs start barking wildly and cockroaches run around like crazy right before a quake," Amy said.

Elizabeth burst out laughing. "Jess, you always did sort of remind me of a roach."

"It says right here in the newspaper that a three-point earthquake on the Richter scale would be *barely* felt by people indoors," Janet said. It was after school on Monday, and she and Lila were hanging out at Lila's house. "Especially if they're on the upper floors of buildings."

"Jessica's bedroom is on the second floor," Lila said. She sat down at the kitchen table and took a sip of lemonade.

"And it would have to be a four- or a five-point one in order for dishes to rattle, and for things to fall over, the way Jessica said they were," Janet went on.

"I knew it," Lila said. "I knew she was lying. She doesn't know what she's talking about. She just wants attention—as usual."

"As usual," Janet agreed.

Lila flipped her long hair over her shoulder. "We need to think of a way to show everybody what a fraud Jessica really is."

"Hmmmm . . ." Janet said thoughtfully. Suddenly she smacked her glass of lemonade on the kitchen table with a bang. "I've got it!"

"What?" Lila asked excitedly.

"Well, Jessica's big thing now is that she thinks she can predict earthquakes," Janet said. "Right?"

Lila smiled. "Right . . ."

"What we do is we get Jessica to predict another earthquake for sure. She can't weasel out of it. After all the bragging she's done, she'll have to make some kind of a prediction. Then she'll look like an idiot when it doesn't happen."

Lila grinned. "So when can we ask the earthquake expert to predict the next big one?"

"You don't actually expect me to *eat* this, do you?" Steven poked at the pot roast in the center of the table with his fork.

Mrs. Wakefield looked at him. "I thought pot roast was one of your favorite meals. You usually eat most of the thing by yourself." She started scooping carrots and potatoes onto her plate from the platter.

"That was before I knew where pot roast came from," Steven said.

"What do you mean?" Elizabeth asked.

"It's beef. It comes from cattle," Steven said.

"Boy genius," Jessica said. "Please pass the salt, Dad."

"Cattle are pumped full of all kinds of pesticides and antibiotics," Steven said, helping himself to some green beans from a separate bowl. "It's really not healthy to eat red meat."

"Well, I agree that it's healthy to cut down and not eat very much of it, but that doesn't mean you have to ban it entirely from your diet," Mr. Wakefield said, putting a slice of roast on Elizabeth's plate.

"I do," Steven said. "I've decided to give up eating all meat, actually."

Mrs. Wakefield dropped her fork onto her plate with a clatter. "What?"

"Are you serious?" Elizabeth asked.

Mr. Wakefield rubbed his ear. "I thought I just heard this young man to my right say he was giving up meat. Could this be my son? The same person who is practically connected by a feeding tube to Hughie's Burger Shack?"

"That was before I knew all the facts about meat," Steven said. "For instance." He pulled a folded sheet of notebook paper out of his pocket. "I've been looking into this stuff all afternoon. Cattle are fed tons of fillers in order to get them up to the right weight—they're even fed *sawdust*. Did you know that? When we eat beef, we're basically eating sawdust. And have you ever seen what happens at a slaughterhouse?"

Jessica stopped slicing her pot roast. "Do you have to tell us this now?"

"Jessica's right, Steven. I'm glad you're interested in this cause, and I think it's a worthy one. But this isn't really the time or the place to go into details," Mrs. Wakefield said. "Why don't we talk about it later."

"OK, have it your way, but *I* wouldn't be filling my body with all those chemicals," Steven said. "I haven't had any meat all day, and I feel fantastic."

"Is that all you're going to eat?" Mr. Wakefield asked. "Green beans and a roll? Just because you don't want any pot roast doesn't mean you shouldn't have a nutritious meal. Is there something else you'd like? How about some tuna fish?"

"No way!" Steven snorted. "I'm giving up fish, too. Hey, do we have any tofu?" he asked in a serious voice.

Jessica had just taken a big sip of milk, and she had to struggle not to spit it out all over the table. "Tofu?" she demanded when she'd finally swallowed. "Steven, do you even know what tofu is?"

"Some kind of bean-curd thing. It's really healthy and also cheap to produce," Steven said with a satisfied expression.

"Well, we don't happen to have any in the fridge right now," Mrs. Wakefield said. "Why don't you make yourself a peanut-butter sandwich? Peanut butter has lots of protein."

"Unless, of course, you don't like the way peanuts are treated," Elizabeth teased him.

"I'm sure the little guys suffer when they're crushed into butter like that," Jessica said, trying not to laugh.

"I don't know—I'll have to look into it," Steven said in a serious voice on his way into the kitchen.

"What's gotten into him?" Mr. Wakefield asked as they listened to Steven fumbling around in the kitchen.

"I don't know, but Steven's not going to last very long on a diet of peanut butter and green beans," Elizabeth said. It was true. Her brother had the biggest appetite of anyone she knew. And almost everything he ate was either a hamburger, a hot dog, or a burrito grande with extra ground beef.

"I don't know if I can even eat this now," Jessica complained, looking at her plate.

"I know," Elizabeth said, staring down at her uneaten meat. Steven came back into the dining room, carrying a peanut butter and sprouts sandwich.

"How about some potatoes and carrots?" Mrs. Wakefield asked, scooping up a serving for him.

Steven shook his head. "They were cooked with the meat, weren't they?"

Mrs. Wakefield just shrugged and put down the spoon she was about to serve him with. "I guess we'll have to do some shopping, and buy you things you like."

"Can you get some sunflower seeds, and lots of beans and rice? Oh yeah, and some of those banana chips, too," Steven said. "And lentils. Don't forget lentils. I read that they're great for vegetarians."

"Whatever you say," Mrs. Wakefield said with a forced smile.

"Better get him some tree bark, too," Jessica said, and Elizabeth laughed.

"Laugh if you want, but *I'm* doing something very important," Steven said. "Of course, I don't expect you little pea-brains to understand."

"Don't worry, Steven, we *never* understand you," Jessica retorted.

Five

◇

"I don't think I've ever seen the sun come up before," Amy said, staring out Elizabeth's bedroom window Tuesday morning at two A.M.

"Well, we have about four more hours until that happens," Elizabeth reminded her. "What else can we do to stay awake?" She was standing in her closet doorway. She and Amy had just tried on almost every single piece of clothing in it.

"We could watch TV," Amy suggested.

"That makes me too sleepy," Elizabeth said.

"We could play some music," Amy said. "That would wake us up."

"Yeah, and it would wake up everyone else in the house too," Elizabeth said. "You know what? We don't *both* have to stay up."

"That's true," Amy said. "We can do this in

shifts—like they do in war movies."

"Yeah, one person keeps watch for a few hours, and then the other person has to," Elizabeth said, nodding. "Let's do that or else we'll both be zombies tomorrow."

"OK, who wants to take the first shift?" Amy asked.

Elizabeth didn't say anything. She wanted more than anything just to fall into her bed and not wake up until it was time for school in the morning. But she didn't want to be selfish. She was the one who'd insisted to Amy that they stay up for the next earthquake. "I'll take the first shift," Elizabeth finally volunteered.

"Are you sure?" Amy asked.

Elizabeth nodded. "Yeah. I'll be fine." She went into the bathroom and splashed some cold water on her face. When she came back out, Amy was facedown on her bed, already asleep.

Elizabeth sat at her desk and got out her math homework. *Maybe if I do some word problems, it'll keep me awake.* She looked at the first one. "Mrs. Jones needs eight hours of sleep. If she falls asleep at ten, and wakes up three separate times for periods of twelve, fifteen, and three minutes, how late should she sleep?"

Elizabeth slammed the book shut and put her head on her desk. What were the chances that the next earthquake would strike in the next four hours? she wondered as she closed her eyes.

"Mom, you should really think about giving up meat too," Steven said when he sat down at breakfast the next morning.

"Really? Why is that?" Mrs. Wakefield asked.

"It's a well-known fact that vegetarians don't get that bone disease old people get, you know, the one where you shrink," Steven said. "Osteo-something."

"Osteoporosis," Mrs. Wakefield said. "Thank you for including me in the old people category."

"No offense, Mom," Steven said. "Just trying to help. I learned a lot from all those brochures Mr. Wheaton gave me."

"Terrific," Mr. Wakefield said. "Now, would you please pass the butter?"

Jessica looked at Elizabeth and Amy and smiled. There was nothing she loved better than seeing her big brother get into trouble.

Steven reached for the butter. Then he looked around the breakfast table and groaned. "There's nothing here I can eat!"

"What do you mean? The only thing you *can't* eat is the bacon," Mr. Wakefield said. "The rest is meatless."

"It's not just the meat, Dad," Steven said, looking at his father as if he were too dumb to understand.

"I mean, I wouldn't even consider putting something like those sugar-frosted flakes in my body. Not to mention those chocolate doughnuts." He picked up the box and read the ingredients out loud. "I mean—'Contains one or more of the following'? The people who *make* these don't know what's in them."

Jessica set down the doughnut she had eaten half of. "Stop it!" she yelled.

"Look, they have beef fat in them!" Steven said. "They can't even make *doughnuts* without killing animals."

"How about some scrambled eggs," Mrs. Wakefield suggested. "I'll make you an omelet filled with vegetables."

Steven shook his head. "Eggs come from chickens."

"Gee, you *have* been reading," Jessica commented.

Amy and Elizabeth started giggling.

"Laugh all you want," Steven said, "but lots of hens die every year from the cruel way they're treated. They get diseases, and then they're turned into—"

"All right, Steven, I've heard more than enough." Mr. Wakefield set down the slice of bacon he'd been about to put into his mouth. "If you don't want to eat this food, fine, but please don't ruin it for the rest of us."

"OK. Fine," Steven said, getting up from the table. "But whatever you do, stay away from the—"

"*Steven!*" Mrs. Wakefield shouted.

"I'm going, I'm going."

"Give me a break!" Jessica complained once he had left the room. "I'm going to school hungry, thanks to him." She threw down her napkin and pushed her chair back from the table.

"I don't want animals to be mistreated either," Elizabeth said. "But what's so bad about my cereal?"

"I'm surprised he didn't yell at me for drinking orange juice," Mrs. Wakefield complained.

"Wait a few minutes and he probably will," Jessica told her.

"Yeah, *Dead Times Two* was a great movie," Mary Wallace was saying on Tuesday morning as the Unicorns stood outside on the steps of school. "I want to see it again."

"Maybe we can go this weekend," Jessica said.

"I can't wait for the sequel," Tamara said. "I wonder if they'll call it *Dead Times Three*."

Suddenly Ellen jabbed Jessica in the ribs. "Look out."

"What?" Jessica demanded.

Just then Lloyd appeared at Jessica's side. He'd come up behind her before she noticed him and had a chance to hide. She tried to look intensely involved in the conversation, but Lloyd walked right up to Jessica and made a sort of snorting noise. "Jessica, I've been researching the fault lines under Sweet Valley."

"Talk about a fault line," Lila muttered under her breath. "Look at how short his pants are."

"It's not how short they are, it's the color," Janet whispered back. Lloyd's pants were made of some mysterious shiny brown and orange material.

"I was wondering if you'd like to have lunch with me today, so we could discuss our strategy," Lloyd said.

"Uh . . . what strategy?" Jessica asked.

"To determine when the next seismic movements will occur," Lloyd said.

"That's right—Jessica can predict earthquakes!" Lila said in an overly energetic voice that sounded phony to Jessica. "Or at least, she *pretends* she can." Lila stared straight at Jessica with a smirk on her face that said *you're a big liar and we all know it*.

"Jessica has demonstrated a unique talent," Lloyd said.

"It wouldn't be the first time," Janet said.

Jessica felt herself getting angrier and angrier. Who were they to tell her she couldn't predict earthquakes? She was getting pretty sick and tired of everyone teasing her. *They* hadn't even woken up during it—what did they know?

"So when can we get together to outline our project?" Lloyd asked.

"I'll get back to you," Jessica said. She hurried into school, leaving Lloyd staring after her and the Unicorns giggling.

Steven stood in the lunch line, trying to decide what to eat. "There really aren't many choices for vegetarians here," he said to Joe, who was in line behind him. "I think I'll talk to Mr. Cooper about it."

Joe shrugged. "Why don't you bring your own lunch?"

"Good idea," Steven said, nodding.

"Look, there's some vegetables," Joe said. "And maybe they have spaghetti sauce without meatballs."

Steven selected a bowl of broccoli—the smell of broccoli made him queasy, but it *was* healthy—and approached the lunch servers. "Do you have any plain spaghetti sauce?" he asked.

"Sure do." One of the kitchen staff put a clump of spaghetti onto a plate and drizzled sauce over it. "Here you go."

Steven took the plate from him and looked at it suspiciously. "Is this meatless sauce?"

"Far as I know," the man replied, shrugging.

Steven studied the sauce. "I think this has some meat in it," he said, pointing to a small bit of hamburger. "Don't you have any that's just tomato?"

"Here." The server handed Steven a plate of plain spaghetti with nothing on it. The pasta had dried out and it stuck together in a hard clump. "Enjoy. Now get moving—there's lots of hungry people behind you."

Steven glared back at the server and put both plates back on the buffet. Then he sat down at a table with Joe.

"Broccoli? That's all you're having?" Joe asked.

"No, I got some bread and crackers, too," Steven said.

"You want a glass of water with that?" Joe teased.

"Don't laugh. Water is very good for you, and it's an important resource," Steven said. "Did you know that it takes less water to feed a total vegetarian for a year than it does to feed a meat-eater for a month?"

"Another fascinating factoid," Joe said, shaking his head. "Please, no more nutrition lectures. All I was saying was it's fine to give up meat and all, but you don't have to eat like you're in jail."

"It's not my fault the school doesn't have good vegetarian food," Steven said, his eyes fixated on Joe's plate. "I can't believe you're going to eat all those meatballs."

Joe looked up at him, a meatball stuck to the end

of his fork. "Don't start telling me what to eat, okay?"

Steven shrugged. "I just thought you'd want to know that you're poisoning yourself. I mean, do you even know how they make ground beef? It's a— Hey, where are you going?"

Joe pushed his chair back from the table and stood up. Then he picked up his tray and walked to the other side of the cafeteria.

Steven sat alone in the crowded lunchroom, staring down into his bowl of cold, smelly broccoli. Being a vegetarian was turning out to be tougher than he'd thought. But he was going to stick with it, even if it meant eating cold broccoli by himself. *That's what it's like, being a crusader for animal rights*, he thought proudly.

"I'm surprised Lloyd didn't follow us here," Janet said as she, Ellen, Lila, Mandy, and Jessica sat down at a table in Casey's Ice Cream Parlor with their sundaes and ice-cream cones.

"We must have ditched him somehow," Jessica said. *He's probably working on his project*, she thought.

"Well, he'll be back," Lila said. "You can bet on that."

"Yeah, he's really convinced you're some kind of scientific discovery," Mandy said.

Jessica just shrugged and took a bite of her sundae. She'd rather not talk about the earthquake, if she could help it. She'd taken enough grief about it already that morning.

"If Lloyd thinks you can predict earthquakes, like you said, then it must really be true," Lila said. She stared at Jessica.

"Whatever," Jessica said casually.

"So, since you say you have this special power, I was wondering when you think the next one will be," Janet said. She licked her strawberry frozen-yogurt cone.

"It'd be great if we knew before everyone else," Ellen said, "so we could plan and everything."

"Well . . . there might be another one," Jessica said. She tried to remember some of the facts she'd read in the library book Elizabeth had. "Maybe later in the week. I'm not sure."

"What do you mean, you're not sure? I thought you could tell when the last one was coming," Lila challenged her.

Jessica pushed the hot fudge around in her sundae glass. "I had this strange feeling the night before, but—"

"So when is it going to be?" Janet asked.

"Yeah, what day?" Lila added.

"I can't tell for sure yet," Jessica said.

"You said you could predict earthquakes," Lila argued. "Can you or can't you?"

Jessica took a deep breath. If Lila was going to be such a jerk about it, there was only one thing to do—bluff. "OK. I didn't want to tell you guys, because I knew you'd get worried, but . . . it's . . . well, it's going to be this Thursday."

"Thursday? You mean, two days from today, right?" Lila asked.

"Yeah. Well, either Thursday or Friday," Jessica said with a nervous smile. That gave her a better chance of being right.

"Which one is it? I mean, if you can *sense* them and all, you should be able to get the day right, at least," Lila said.

Jessica glared back at her. "Thursday," she said, more confidently this time.

"Great!" Lila exclaimed.

"What do you mean, great?" Ellen asked. "When can an earthquake be great?"

"When I have a special Earthquake Party, that's when," Lila said, grinning.

"What? A party?" Jessica asked.

"Yeah, I've been thinking about it ever since yesterday," Lila said. "And now, thanks to your special sensitivity, I can make up the invitations and set the date. I'm going to invite everyone, so we can all experience it together this time."

"B-but how do you know exactly *when* it's going to be? It might happen when we're all at school,"

Jessica pointed out nervously.

"No problem," Lila said. "I'll just count on your special powers to let us know exactly when it's going to hit. You can do that, can't you?"

Jessica swallowed hard.

"We should decorate your basement with all kinds of earthquake stuff," Janet said.

"We can serve shakes," Lila suggested.

"And dance the bump," Mandy added, laughing.

"That's a great idea," Ellen said.

Jessica cleared her throat. "You know, Thursday's a school night. Do you think people will be able to come?"

"It's only the event of the century," Janet said. "They'll come."

"Yeah, and I know someone who'll be there early," Lila said, nodding toward the door.

Lloyd had just walked in. Jessica tried to sink down in her seat, but it was too late.

"Hi, Jessica," Lloyd said. His briefcase made a clinking noise when he set it on the floor.

"Hi," Jessica said.

"How do you feel?" he asked, pulling up a chair. "What's your reading of the seismic activity this afternoon?"

"Oh, Jessica has big news," Lila said with a smirk. "She says there's going to be another quake on Thursday."

"Really?" Lloyd sat up straighter in his chair. "That's incredible!"

What's incredible is the huge, stupid mess I'm in, Jessica thought.

Six

"Steven, we've been talking about your plan to become a vegetarian, and we want to clear up a few things with you," Mr. Wakefield said when Steven came into the kitchen early that evening. Elizabeth was sitting at the kitchen table doing her homework while her parents unpacked groceries.

"I'm not a vegetarian, I'm a vegan," Steven said.

"A what?" Jessica asked.

"A vegan," Steven said. "It means I eat only plant foods— no animal foods, eggs, or dairy products. And I don't buy any wool or leather, because they come from animals too."

"Hmm. So it looks like you'll be throwing out your new leather ultimate basketball sneakers," Mrs. Wakefield said.

Steven looked as if he hadn't considered doing that. "Oh. Yeah, right," he said.

"We can give them to Goodwill—I'm sure someone else can use them," Mr. Wakefield said. "You'll have to get a pair of canvas ones."

"OK," Steven said uncertainly.

"Now, about your eating—" Mrs. Wakefield began.

"Don't try to talk me out of it," Steven interrupted. "My mind's made up."

"Oh, we're not going to try to stop you," Mrs. Wakefield said.

"Yeah, we think it's a really fantastic idea," Elizabeth said.

"You do?" Steven looked surprised.

"Sure," Elizabeth said. "Actually, you're really inspiring." She smiled at him.

"I am?" Steven asked.

"And that's why we've decided to help you as much as we can," Mrs. Wakefield said. "I stopped by the supermarket on the way home from work and picked up lots of things for you. Actually, it was pretty interesting—I got into a conversation with the clerk, and she told me there have been lots of famous vegetarians—like Socrates, and Leonardo da Vinci."

"Wow, I didn't know that," Elizabeth said. "That's cool."

"And tonight we'll be having a completely

meat-free meal," Mr. Wakefield said. "We've got a nice tofu-and-vegetable stir fry planned for tonight."

"And I bought some whole-grain bread and some soy milk—"

"What's that?" Steven asked.

"Well, you want to eliminate dairy products from your diet, right? It's milk made from soybeans," Mr. Wakefield explained.

"Yum," Elizabeth said, laughing.

"Great," Steven said, nodding seriously.

The door opened and Jessica walked in. "Hi," she said in a tired voice.

"Where have you been?" asked Elizabeth.

"I was at Casey's," Jessica replied, sinking into a chair at the kitchen table.

"What did you have?" Steven asked.

"The usual. A hot-fudge sundae with peanut-butter-cup ice cream, extra whipped cream, and marshmallow topping," Jessica said. "Why?"

Elizabeth expected Steven to go into another lecture about the evils of eating dairy products. Instead he sighed loudly. "Just wondering," he said.

Jessica pressed the channel button on the remote control. She wanted to watch a few minutes of television before she went to bed, but there was nothing on. Just a bunch of boring movies and reruns of old sitcoms. She curled up on the couch and lazily watched the local late-night news.

She was almost asleep when she heard the word "earthquake." She bolted up on the couch and turned up the volume.

A reporter was interviewing an earthquake expert from San Francisco. The seismologist was standing in a lab full of machines that made graphs, and other strange-looking equipment. "In my opinion, the chances for another earthquake in the Sweet Valley area are extremely slim," she said. "A few aftershocks still may occur, but nothing even the most practiced seismologist would feel."

Jessica's right eyebrow arched. "No," she said out loud, "don't tell me that." *Lloyd doesn't know what he's talking about!* she thought, panicking. *And now* I'm *the one who's going to pay for it.*

Jessica was almost glad when the interview was over a minute later. She didn't know how much more bad news she could take. Lila was planning an Earthquake Party because of her, and more than likely, there wasn't going to *be* any earthquake.

Then she thought about it for a second. Where had this earthquake expert been the night before Monday morning's earthquake? Had *she* felt funny the night before? Had *she* woken up during it? No.

Anyway, there were lots of things scientists didn't know. For example, they couldn't explain

UFOs, or ESP, or ghosts. They didn't know *everything*.

"What are you doing here?" Jessica asked a few minutes later, walking into Elizabeth's bedroom.

"It's nice to see you, too," Amy replied.

"What I mean is, how come you get to sleep over *again*? On a school night? Mom hardly ever lets us do that—and you get to do it twice in a row?" Jessica said.

"Amy and I are working on something special for school," Elizabeth said. "Didn't I tell you about our earthquake project?"

Jessica rolled her eyes. "I'm not so sure I want to hear about it."

"We're going to stay up all night for the next few days, so that if there's another earthquake, we won't miss it," Elizabeth explained.

"You are?" Jessica asked. "So you think there's going to be another one . . . soon?" She sounded almost hopeful to Elizabeth.

"It's possible," Amy said. "And if it happens, we want to be awake this time. We want to write about it for the *Sixers*, as part of our big earthquake article."

"So Amy's going to be sleeping over for the next few nights," Elizabeth told her twin. "I don't know how we'll stay up all night, but we'll manage somehow. Mr. Bowman kind of dared us. He told us if we wanted to do an article, we had to witness the next earthquake."

"We're sleeping in shifts," Amy explained. "What about you, Jessica? Do you want to stay up too?"

"No way!" Jessica said quickly.

"Oh. That's right. I guess you don't have to," Amy teased. "I mean, you'll just automatically wake up when it happens."

"I probably will," Jessica said, sounding irritated.

"Have you sensed when it'll happen again?" Elizabeth asked. She smiled at Amy when Jessica didn't answer right away. "Or have you given up on your special powers?"

Jessica glared at her. "As a matter of fact, I was telling Lila earlier that I think there might be another quake on Thursday."

Elizabeth's eyebrows shot up in surprise. "Are you serious?"

"Of course, I don't know for sure," Jessica added.

Amy shot her a suspicious look.

"But I'm pretty sure," Jessica said quickly. "In fact, almost positive."

"Whatever you say," Elizabeth said, shrugging. "You're the expert. Speaking of which, I forgot to tell you that Lloyd called tonight while you were taking a shower."

*   *   *

Steven lay awake and stared at the ceiling. He listened to his stomach moan and grumble. He was starving. He felt as if he hadn't eaten anything in two days. Which wasn't completely true: he'd picked at spinach, broccoli, sprouts—even tofu. It was *worse* than nothing. Just the thought of some of the things he'd eaten made him feel sick.

Visions of double cheeseburgers with bacon on top floated through Steven's mind. His mouth watered. He couldn't help it. Then he thought about the video, and the books he'd read. They did have important things to say. He wanted to go along with all their recommendations.

Besides, now that everyone knew he was trying to be a vegetarian, he couldn't just give up after only two days. He'd be humiliated. His parents had said they were proud of him, and they'd gone out and bought all those special kinds of food. Elizabeth had actually called him inspiring.

Joe and Cathy would never let Steven live it down if he went to the cafeteria tomorrow and started eating meat again, after all the things he'd preached to Joe about his new crusade.

Did I actually call it a crusade? Steven wondered, his stomach growling loudly as he turned onto his side.

Why did I have to open my big mouth?

Seven

"Only one more day until the earthquake," Ellen said on Wednesday morning. The Unicorns—all except Jessica, who was late as usual—had gotten together in the art studio a half hour before school. "I can't believe it. I wonder how big it will be."

"You don't actually think there's going to *be* one, do you?" Janet said, adding the finishing touches to Lila's party invitations. She drew the word "SHAKE" in big block letters, making them look as though they were made out of stone.

"We're just doing this to prove Jessica was lying," Lila said.

"I'm not so sure she was lying," Ellen said, slipping the finished invitation into the photocopy machine so they could print copies. "I mean, I kind of believe her."

Lila looked at Janet and shook her head. "If Jessica told you she could predict a hurricane, or a tornado, would you believe that?" she asked Ellen.

Ellen shrugged and pressed a button on the copy machine. "If she had evidence that she could. And she *is* the only person we know who even felt the earthquake."

Just then Jessica walked into the room. "Sorry I'm late," she said. "I overslept."

"I guess she couldn't *sense* that it was time to get up," Janet whispered to Lila, who laughed.

"That's okay—we're done already," Tamara said, pulling a copy of the invitation out of the copy-machine tray. "See?" She handed it to Jessica.

"That looks great," Mary said. "The artwork came out really well."

Lila watched Jessica study the invitation. She wasn't saying anything. "Make a hundred and fifty copies," Lila instructed Ellen.

"What?" Jessica cried, dropping the invitation. It fluttered to the floor. "A hundred and fifty?"

"I want this to be a big party," Lila said. "It's going to be a major event."

"But—I thought this was a Unicorn party," Jessica said, looking flustered.

"It *is* a Unicorn party—we're hosting it for everyone," Janet said. "Don't the invitations look fantastic?" She started stacking the copies.

"We can hand them out in all our classes this morning." Mary divided the stack into separate piles, one for each of them.

"You know," Jessica said with a casual wave of her hand, "maybe having a party on the day of the earthquake isn't such a good idea."

"What do you mean? It's a great idea," Lila insisted.

"Well . . . I'd just feel really awful if it was a strong earthquake, and somebody got hurt or something," Jessica said. She frowned, a serious expression on her face.

What an actress, Lila thought. "Really?" she said.

"Maybe we should all stay home, just in case," Jessica continued. "We'd be safer that way."

"We'll be perfectly safe," Lila said firmly. "The party's going to be in our huge, earthquake-resistant basement."

"Yeah, nothing bad's going to happen," Mary said.

"Anyway, if it was going to be a severe earthquake, you'd probably be having some strong feelings already, instead of the kind of *uncertain* ones you've been experiencing," Lila pointed out.

"They're not uncertain!" Jessica insisted. "I told you the earthquake would be Thursday, and it'll happen on Thursday."

Lila looked right into Jessica's eyes. "All I can

say is, after all the work we're doing for my party, there'd *better* be an earthquake," she said.

"Hi, Jessica. I have great news," Lloyd said, coming up to her at her locker later that morning.

You decided to leave me alone? Jessica said to herself.

"I got my dad to lend me his beeper," he said, handing Jessica a phone number on a slip of paper. "Now you can contact me anytime, whenever you feel the slightest tremor. Since you think the next one's coming tomorrow, I wanted us to be in touch at all times."

"That's really not necessary," Jessica said, frowning. The only tremors she was feeling were from her nerves. "Lloyd, can I ask you something? Do *you* think there might be an earthquake this week?" Jessica asked nervously.

Lloyd bowed. "I defer to you. You're the expert."

Jessica shook her head. "No, I'm not."

"How can you say that?" Lloyd looked confused. "You've predicted another quake for Thursday— isn't that true?"

Jessica shrugged. "Yeah, I guess."

"When did you feel it coming?"

When Lila made me say it was coming, Jessica thought with a sigh. "The other day, remember? Listen, I have to go to lunch. I'll talk to you about it later," she said.

"All right, but let me know if you feel anything coming," Lloyd said. "Oh—and I wanted to tell you, I've been working on something for our project that's really exciting. We're going to make scientific history together."

"Can't wait," Jessica said glumly, walking down the hall.

"One of the major safety rules for earthquakes is to stay in a safe place," Jessica told Aaron and Todd at lunch. She was walking from table to table, trying to convince people to stay away from Lila's party.

"What's safer than Lila's basement?" Aaron asked. "I'm sure her father had the house built to withstand earthquakes." Mr. Fowler was very rich, and he was known for sparing no expense.

"Maybe, but . . . what if too many people show up, and there's one of those mass-panic scenes?" Jessica asked.

"There won't be," Todd said confidently. "No one's going to panic."

"Yeah, I can't wait to see this earthquake," Aaron said. "That's really cool, how you can predict them, Jessica."

Really cool, Jessica thought as she walked over to where Bruce Patman was sitting with his friends. *More like really dumb.* "Hi," she said, smiling at

Bruce. "Did you get the invitation to Lila's party?"

"Yeah, and I'm psyched," Bruce said. "I'm actually going to make some money off this."

"How?" Jessica frowned.

"I'm having T-shirts printed up, and I'm going to sell them at the party. See?" He handed Jessica a napkin with a sketch of a T-shirt on it. One side said I SURVIVED THE BIG ONE and the other side had Thursday's date printed on it. "What do you think? Pretty impressive, huh?"

"Yeah," Jessica said, handing the napkin back to him. "That's great. Just great." She had a sinking feeling *she* wasn't going to survive the party. "How many are you going to get?" she asked Bruce.

"Oh, about a hundred," Bruce said. "I figure everyone will want one—it's a great earthquake souvenir to remember the big day."

Sure, if there was going to be anything to remember, Jessica thought dejectedly. She grabbed an apple and went to sit in the Unicorner for the last few minutes of the lunch period.

"Everyone's talking about our party," Lila told her when she sat down. "Already forty-two people have told me they'll definitely be there."

"On a school night?" Jessica said. "How can that many people be allowed to go out on a school night?"

Lila smiled. "It's a special event, remember? And we have you to thank for it."

Jessica crunched into her apple. "You're welcome," she muttered.

"I'll have the jumbo bacon burger, a large order of onion rings, and a mocha milk shake. And don't say anything." Joe frowned at Steven.

"I wasn't going to," Steven protested. "You can eat whatever you want." He scanned the menu. "I'll have . . ." *Everything on the menu*, he wanted to say. "Just some fries, please."

"How are the fries cooked—what kind of oil?" Joe asked.

"Uh . . . cottonseed oil, I think," the waiter said.

Joe shook his head. "You can't get that, Steven. It's too unhealthy."

Steven gritted his teeth. "Then how about a garden salad," he said. "With oil and vinegar dressing."

"Better make it just vinegar," Joe told the waiter. "He's on a very restricted diet."

Steven glared at him.

"So are you going to play that pickup basketball game tonight?" Joe asked. "It should be great."

Steven shrugged. Since he'd given up meat, he didn't feel as if he had the energy to do much of anything. "I don't know. Maybe."

"Some guys from Big Mesa are coming—remember the center who practically killed us last game? He scored something like forty points," Joe said. "I heard he'll be there."

Steven didn't answer. At the moment he was suddenly overcome with all the wonderful smells inside the restaurant. Hamburgers and chicken on the grill . . . and the girls at the table beside him were eating butterscotch and hot-fudge sundaes. He stared at a boy eating a pork rib dripping with barbecue sauce.

Joe snapped his fingers in front of Steven's face. "Are you listening to me or what?"

"Sorry," Steven said. "What were you saying?"

"Never mind—here comes our food," Joe answered.

The waiter set down Joe's plate, with onion rings heaped all over his jumbo bacon burger. Then he put a small salad plate in front of Steven. "I put the dressing on the side, because of your special diet," he said with a smile.

Steven resisted the urge to throw the small container of vinegar back in the waiter's face.

"Man, I'm starved." Joe took a big bite of his burger. Steven watched his jaw move up and down, transfixed.

Then he looked at the salad. Salads weren't exactly a strong point on the Dairi Burger menu. It was mostly just some hamburger toppings thrown together—a wilted mix of lettuce, tomato, and onion. Steven put some vinegar drops on top of it and started to eat.

"Hey, there's Chuck Harmon—I need to ask him something about tonight's game. I'll be right back." Joe put his burger on the plate and wiped his hands on a napkin.

As soon as he was gone, Steven went back to staring at the hamburger. He glanced around the restaurant. Joe's back was facing him as he leaned over a booth to talk to Chuck. There was nobody else around to see him cheat. He could take one little bite and put it back before Joe was finished talking to Chuck.

He stared at the burger again. *Do you really want to do that?* he asked himself.

He reached across the table.

"Ha!" Joe cried. "Caught you!"

Steven jumped up guiltily and took his hands off the hamburger bun. "I wasn't going to eat it."

"Really?" Joe sat down. "It sure looked that way."

"No, I was just . . . well, actually, I was thinking that if the Dairi Burger started ordering some whole-grain buns, that burger would be much better for you," Steven said, stabbing his salad with his fork.

Joe nodded and grinned. "Yeah. Exactly what I was thinking." He picked up the burger and took another jumbo bite.

Eight

◇

"Where should I put this?" Lila held up a poster of a giant crack in the earth. It was an overhead photo of the San Andreas Fault that she'd borrowed from Mr. Seigel's office earlier that afternoon.

"How about over here?" Janet pointed to a spot on the wall, near where the table of food would be.

"What did you finally decide to serve for food, anyway?" Mary asked Lila.

"Milk shakes and rock candy," Lila said, tacking the poster to the wall in her basement. It wasn't a normal basement, because Lila's house was huge—more like a mansion than a house. The basement was as large as the entire first floor, and it was almost as nice. Lila used it frequently for parties.

"And we're making a huge sheet cake tonight at my house," Janet said, hanging some inflatable globes from the ceiling. "We're frosting it to look like Sweet Valley, and then we're going to cut it in half with a jagged knife, so it splits."

"That sounds really cool," Mandy said. "Don't you think so, Jessica?" She was filling small flashlights with batteries and setting them on small end tables all around the basement.

Jessica was sitting on a chair in the corner. "Yeah." She sighed.

"Hey, Jessica, can you help me with this?" Janet asked. "I need someone to pass me the tape."

Lila watched as Jessica half walked and half dragged herself over to Janet, who was standing on a chair. "Where's the tape?" she asked.

"Right there." Janet pointed to the table.

Jessica grabbed the roll of tape and started handing Janet little pieces of it.

"So, Jessica," Lila began. "Since it's almost Wednesday night, have you sensed anything yet?"

"Yeah, do you have that funny feeling you got before the last one?" Mandy asked.

"No," Jessica said.

"Uh-oh," Lila said. "Does that mean it's not going to happen?"

"No," Jessica said, frowning. "It just means that I'm not sure exactly when yet."

"When do you think you'll know?" asked Janet. "Later tonight?"

"Why does it matter, anyway?" Jessica asked, sounding aggravated.

"Well, we don't want to do all this work for nothing," Mandy said.

"It'd be a real shame if everyone showed up and the earthquake happened after they left, or Friday or next week or something," Lila said. "I don't want to host a loser party. I'd hate it if everyone blamed *you* because they had a bad time."

Jessica ripped off another piece of Scotch tape. "It'll happen tomorrow, all right? I said it would, and it will."

Lila smiled. If Jessica wanted to dig a deeper hole for herself, she was doing a pretty good job.

"So how's the vegetarian plan going?" Mr. Wakefield asked Steven as he set the table for dinner Wednesday night.

"OK, I guess," Steven said. He was slumped on the couch in the living room, watching television. A commercial came on advertising a new steak sauce, and Steven quickly changed the channel.

"I experimented a little and cooked something new tonight," Mr. Wakefield said. "I got a great vegetarian cookbook, with some very healthy recipes. I think you'll like this one."

Steven swallowed a sip of spring water. For some reason he didn't think he was going to agree with his father. "What is it?" he asked, dreading the answer.

"It's mushroom-tofu-pecan stuffed squash. Doesn't it smell fantastic? I'd better check on it." Mr. Wakefield set down the last fork and went back into the kitchen.

Steven groaned silently and rolled over on the couch.

"Hey, what's on?" Jessica asked, coming downstairs. She sank onto the couch beside him.

"Nothing," Steven grumbled.

"What's your problem?" Jessica asked.

"Nothing," Steven said. "Just leave me alone."

"Maybe you should start eating more meat," she said, giving him a strange look. "You're turning into a real grouch."

Steven glared at her. "It's not because of that, stupid."

"Fine, *don't* talk to me. It's not like I need more aggravation in my life." Jessica folded her arms and the two of them watched TV in silence until Mr. Wakefield called them for dinner a few minutes later.

"This is a side dish called taboule," Mr. Wakefield told everyone as soon as they'd sat down. He passed the bowl to Elizabeth.

Elizabeth took a small bite to test it. "Wow, this is really good," she said enthusiastically. "I like the lemon flavor."

Steven put a clump of taboule on his plate, then

took a bite. It tasted like mashed-up cardboard to him. *What* lemon? he wanted to say.

"Thanks for having me for dinner," Amy said. "I love this squash."

"You're welcome, and thanks for the compliment," Mr. Wakefield said with a grin. "Try the Middle Eastern carrot salad."

"Ned, I think you've found your calling," Steven's mother said. "Everything's delicious."

"Are you saying it's time for me to give up being a lawyer, and open my own vegetarian restaurant?" Mr. Wakefield asked, still smiling.

Steven poked at the squash, then took a small bite. He hated squash.

"Steven, I'm so glad you decided to give up meat," his mother said. "It's given us all the opportunity to rethink our diet."

"You're welcome," Steven said, staring down at his plate.

"Yeah, you really inspired me," his father added. "It's good for all of us to eat less meat. Of course, we don't have to give it up entirely, but then, we're not as dedicated as you."

Steven frowned.

"I'm impressed," said Elizabeth. "I have to say, I really didn't think you could do it. Usually when you try stuff, you give up right away. But it's already been three days."

"I know," Steven muttered. *Boy, do I know.*

"Remember when you said you were going to work out three times a day, and you gave up on the second day?" Jessica asked.

"How about when you said you were going to do your homework every day before six o'clock—*that* only lasted a day," Elizabeth said.

"Well, Steven's not going to give up this time. He's committed to a cause," Mr. Wakefield said. "Right, Steven?"

"Yeah, right," Steven said. He washed down the carrot salad with a gulp of spring water. Why did they have to be so supportive *now*? Steven wondered. Couldn't they at least try to talk him out of it?

"Jessica's still going with her Thursday prediction—I can't believe it," Amy said later that night as she and Elizabeth sat on her bedroom floor, playing cards.

Elizabeth yawned. It was almost midnight. After staying up most of the night before, she was exhausted. "Well, for both our sakes, I hope she's right. I don't know how many more nights I can stay up."

"Maybe we'll be lucky and it'll happen really soon," Amy said. "Like, anytime in the next ten minutes would be great."

"I wouldn't count on it." Elizabeth put down a card.

Amy sighed. "This is probably pretty pointless."

Elizabeth sighed too. "I have a feeling you're right. But let's just try to stick it out another day just in case."

"OK, but I'm sick of cards. What else can we do?"

"We could read," Elizabeth suggested.

"OK."

Elizabeth got out a book they were reading for English class and leaned back against her bed. Amy lay down on the bed after picking out an Amanda Howard mystery from Elizabeth's bookshelves.

A few minutes later Elizabeth heard a snore. She turned around. Amy was facedown on the bed, her head buried in the pillow, fast asleep. "Great. Now I have to stay up by myself," Elizabeth mumbled. She really wasn't looking forward to it.

She got up and went downstairs to the kitchen. She decided to make herself some coffee. She'd only ever had little sips of her parents' coffee before, but she knew it had caffeine in it, which would keep her awake.

The pot was almost done brewing when Jessica walked into the kitchen.

"What are you doing up?" Elizabeth asked.

"I can't sleep," Jessica said, collapsing into a chair at the kitchen table. "I'm too worried."

"About the earthquake coming?" Elizabeth got a

cup from the cupboard and poured coffee into it.

"About the earthquake *not* coming," Jessica said.

"But I thought you were so sure it would happen today," Elizabeth said, dumping spoonfuls of sugar into the coffee. Then she added a lot of cream.

Jessica shook her head. "I don't know when it'll come. I don't know *if* it will come." She buried her head in her arms and groaned. "I only predicted it because Lila said I couldn't."

"And she's right—you can't," Elizabeth said.

"I know, but Lila didn't have to *say* that," Jessica said, pouting.

"Well, it might happen tomorrow," Elizabeth said. "There's always a chance. And if you are right, Amy and I will get a great article out of it."

"Yeah, but if I'm not right, I'm going to be totally, completely humiliated. *Publicly* humiliated." Jessica gave her a pitiful look.

Elizabeth took a sip of the coffee. She had to force herself to swallow it. "I think I made this too strong," she told Jessica, making a face. "Do you want to stay up with me? Amy fell asleep already."

"Elizabeth!" Jessica cried. "Don't you even care?"

"Sure, but there's nothing you or I can do about it now," Elizabeth said with a shrug. "It'll either happen or it won't."

"Oh, thanks. Thanks a lot," Jessica said. "Next time you need help, don't ask *me*." She stood up and marched up the stairs to her room.

Elizabeth took another sip of coffee and shook her head. Life with Jessica was never boring, but it could be pretty irritating sometimes.

Nine

Jessica went down to breakfast the next morning feeling completely exhausted. She'd tossed and turned all night, worrying about what would happen today. She'd even dreamed that while she was sitting in school, an earthquake had toppled the entire building. It was a good dream, actually. At least there had been an earthquake.

Maybe that dream means it will come today after all, she thought. She was at the bottom of the stairs when she saw Steven in the kitchen, reaching for something in the refrigerator. She was surprised to see him pull out the carton of milk. He wasn't supposed to eat any dairy products at all.

She waited for him to pour it. She couldn't wait to catch him in the act.

Steven opened the spout and lifted the carton.

But just as he was about to pour it, his father opened the kitchen door and walked in. "That paperboy with the bad aim threw our newspaper clear into the neighbor's yard this time," Mr. Wakefield complained, shaking out the *Sweet Valley Tribune*. "I'm going to have to talk to him."

Rats, Jessica thought as Steven hurriedly shoved the milk carton back into the refrigerator before her father noticed. Steven took out the container of soy milk and sloshed some onto his bowl of granola. He looked as though he was about to cry.

Jessica smiled. *Somehow I get the feeling his vegetarian plan isn't going to last much longer.*

"Elizabeth, wake up!" Amy poked Elizabeth in the arm. "We're going to be way late for school."

"What?" Elizabeth sat up and rubbed her eyes. She had fallen asleep with her head on the desk, and her back was all stiff from sleeping in such a cramped position.

"I can't believe you fell asleep—what if we missed the earthquake?" Amy asked, quickly changing clothes.

"*Me?* What about you?" Elizabeth ran to her closet to pick out some clothes. "I stayed up until at least three o'clock. *You* fell asleep right after midnight."

"I couldn't help it," Amy said.

"And you fell asleep the night before, too," Elizabeth said. "I'm sick of being the one who has to stay up by myself."

"All you had to do was wake me up," Amy said, brushing her hair in front of the mirror.

"I tried, but you didn't budge!" Elizabeth said, feeling aggravated.

"Maybe you should have tried harder—it's not my fault!" Amy said.

"Yes, it is!" Elizabeth cried.

There was a knock on the door. "What are you two yelling about?" Mrs. Wakefield asked, poking her head into the room.

"Amy fell asleep again, and we're supposed to be staying up on our earthquake watch," Elizabeth said, pulling a sweater over her head.

"I tried to stay up," Amy said. "I guess I'm just not very good at this."

Elizabeth yawned. "You can say that again."

"Oh, like you stayed up all night?" Amy retorted. "And what about Monday night, when you were supposed to take the first shift and you fell asleep and never even woke me up for *my* shift?"

"Maybe that wouldn't have happened if you'd offered to take the first shift," Elizabeth argued. "But no, *I* had to do it."

Mrs. Wakefield looked from Elizabeth to Amy and laughed. "You guys are only arguing because you're tired. Sleep deprivation can do that to a person. Come on downstairs and have some breakfast, and I'll drop you at school on my way to work so you won't be late."

"At least someone around here is considerate," Elizabeth said.

Amy tossed her dark-blond hair over her shoulder and walked out of the room.

If this earthquake doesn't happen soon, Jessica's not the only person who's going to be sorry! Elizabeth thought, frowning as she followed Amy down the stairs.

"Mr. Bowman, can I make an announcement?" Jessica stood nervously at her English teacher's desk.

"What kind of announcement?" Mr. Bowman asked, straightening his orange striped tie.

"A really important one. You know, kind of like that Emergency Broadcast Signal thing." Jessica smiled her most charming smile.

"All right, but like the Emergency Broadcast Signal test, it should last only sixty seconds," Mr. Bowman said.

Jessica nodded and stood at the front of the classroom as the bell rang. She waited for everyone to take their seats.

"OK, a lot of you guys already know that there might be an earthquake today—er, tonight," Jessica said, glancing at Lila. "Well, as someone with an extra sensitivity to earthquakes—"

A few of the boys in the class snickered.

"I have a feeling that this earthquake could be a strong one," Jessica continued, ignoring them. "Very strong." She tried to look as serious and worried as possible. "And that's why I want to warn people to stay home tonight."

"What?" Ellen cried. "We can't stay home—we're having a party."

Jessica sighed. "I know. But I wouldn't want to be responsible for anyone getting hurt."

"How kind of you," Mr. Bowman said. It was obvious he thought the whole earthquake thing was a hoax. "Now, if you'll just take your seat—"

"I just want people to know how dangerous it is," Jessica said, as Mr. Bowman gestured toward her seat with a chalk eraser. "Everyone should be incredibly careful and stay home tonight unless they absolutely *have* to go out."

"Well, I absolutely *have* to go to that party," Winston said. "I can't wait for the earthcake."

"You mean earthquake," Ellen said.

"No, earthcake," Winston said. "Grace told me about it. Chocolate with green icing."

"Yeah, and I want to buy one of those T-shirts Bruce is selling," Danny Jackson added.

"Well, don't get your hopes up too high," Jessica said. "If the earthquake happens before tonight, Lila might have to call off the party."

"Call it off?" Lila said. "Call it off? I don't think so."

Jessica sat down on the edge of her seat, keeping her distance from Lila.

"It sounds like you don't want people to come to my party," Lila whispered to her. "Now, why would that be?"

"Um . . . I was just thinking, you know, safety first," Jessica whispered back as Mr. Bowman started class. *And then there's my reputation.*

"Elizabeth, oh, Elizabeth!"

Elizabeth was walking up to a large, shining stage, surrounded by crowds and crowds of people in fancy dresses and tuxedos. She blushed and carefully took the steps up onto the stage, making sure she didn't trip on her sparkling evening gown. Everyone was applauding loudly, and some people were shouting her name.

"Earth to Elizabeth!"

"And now, ladies and gentlemen, this year's winner of the Pulitzer Prize for news reporting, Miss Elizabeth—"

"Elizabeth Wakefield!"

Elizabeth jerked awake. She saw Ms. Blake standing in front of her, and realized her entire science class was laughing.

"Cute snore you've got!" Danny called.

"My class isn't *that* boring, is it?" Ms. Blake said.

"N-no," Elizabeth faltered, her cheeks warm. "Sorry. I just haven't been, um, sleeping very well lately."

"Until now, that is!" Belinda added.

"Well, try to catch up on your sleep tonight, OK? Now, would you care to join us for the rest of class?" Ms. Blake asked her, smiling.

Elizabeth looked down at her book. "Sure." She felt so embarrassed. She'd never fallen asleep in the middle of a class before.

"We're on page seventy-eight," Ms. Blake said.

Elizabeth found the right page. But as she stared at the story, all the words on the page started blurring together. *This is all Amy's fault!* she thought, struggling to keep her eyes open.

"She's panicking," Lila told Janet at her locker, in between classes Thursday morning. "She's practically begging everyone not to come to the party."

"I love it," Janet said. "We're going to get her, but good."

"I wonder if she'll even show her face at the party," Lila said, shifting her books in her arms.

"She has to," Janet said. "She made such a big deal out of it, she can't just not show up."

"Well, if I were her, I'd be crawling under a rock right about now," Lila said.

"Hey, what's up?" Aaron asked, walking past.

"Oh, nothing," Lila said, smiling. "We were just talking about the party tonight."

"It'll be so excellent if Jessica turns out to be right," Aaron said.

And even more excellent if she's wrong, Lila thought. *That is*, when *she's wrong*. "Make sure you come early," she told Aaron. "I think there's going to be a lot of people."

"Oh, I know—everyone's going," Aaron said. "See you tonight."

"Bye!" Janet waved to him, then turned back to Lila. "Can you imagine anything more perfect? A house full of people—and no earthquake."

"I don't know. I'm almost starting to feel sorry for Jessica," Lila said. "She's going to be so embarrassed."

Janet stared at her. "What?"

"Just kidding," Lila said. "This is going to be the best party I've ever had."

"I can't believe the Valentine's dance is only a few weeks away," Mandy said later that day in the cafeteria. She and Jessica had arrived at the Unicorner first.

Jessica was glad they were sitting in the corner. She was trying to keep a low profile. "I'm so glad someone wants to talk about something other than the stupid earthquake," she said.

"Do you know who you're going with yet?" Mandy asked.

"Aaron, I guess," Jessica said. "But he hasn't asked me yet. Maybe I'll ask him. Who do you want to go with?"

"Promise you won't tell anyone?" Mandy asked.

"Of course not," Jessica said. "Who?"

"Peter Jeffries," Mandy said. Peter was in the seventh grade. He was very good-looking, and popular, too. He and Mandy had actually gone out together once, but nothing had come of it, and Mandy's crush had just gotten worse. "Do you think I have a chance?"

"Sure, why not?" Jessica said. Suddenly she sensed someone standing at her elbow. She moved her chair over and looked up, expecting to see Grace or Lila.

It was Lloyd, carrying a contraption made of thin plastic tubes and a variety of dials, all attached to a canvas fisherman's vest. "Jessica, this is the surprise I was telling you about."

Jessica's eyes widened.

Lila, Janet, and Grace set their trays on the table and sat down.

"What's that?" Lila asked, wrinkling her nose.

"Is that your new fashion statement, Lloyd?" Janet asked.

"No, it's for Jessica," Lloyd replied.

Everyone turned to Jessica and started giggling. Lila was laughing so hard, Jessica thought she might be choking.

"Very funny, Lloyd," Jessica said, pushing the vest toward him.

"Jessica, you have to wear this," Lloyd insisted, holding it out toward her. "You absolutely must. It's a vital element of our experiment."

Jessica shook her head. "No way."

"Oh, come on, Jessica—you look good in tan," Janet teased.

"Don't you want all the fame and glory that's going to come from our presentation at the state science fair?" Lloyd asked.

"Not if I have to wear that thing, I don't!" Jessica practically exploded.

"But—but what am I going to tell the Center for Earthquake Research?" Lloyd asked, looking genuinely hurt.

"Tell them we're not coming," Jessica snapped.

Lloyd frowned. "But I spent hours on this."

"Look, Lloyd, just leave me alone!" Jessica got up and hurried from the lunchroom. She went out into the hallway and leaned against the wall.

She couldn't believe she had gotten herself into this. She'd been spending so much time talking to Lloyd, everyone was going to think she was a nerd. And after tonight, everyone was going to know she was a liar. A nerdy liar. A lying nerd. What a combination.

There had to be *some* way to get out of this. There had to be. She just hadn't thought of it yet.

She was just turning to go to her locker when she heard footsteps behind her.

"Does this mean we're not going to the seismic research conference next month?" Lloyd asked, coming up beside her, still carrying the vest.

"Can I have a bite of your sandwich?" Steven looked longingly at the barbecue sauce dripping off Cathy's sandwich.

"Steven, it's chicken," Cathy said.

"I know," Steven said. "Just give me a bite. One teeny tiny bite." His mouth watered at the thought.

"Don't you remember what you told me about chicken, after that video?" Cathy asked. "For one thing, they're packed full of antibiotics, unless they're free-range chickens."

"So? Antibiotics aren't that bad," Steven said. "I mean, doctors give them to you when you're sick, right? They can't be all that bad for you." Steven knew he was grasping at straws, but he would do anything he could to talk Cathy into giving him the sandwich. Or a bite, anyway.

"That's not what you said Monday," Cathy reminded him. "You said you weren't going to poison your body ever again."

"That was Monday," Steven grumbled. "It's Thursday now."

"Besides, what about the cruel way they're treated?" Cathy said. "Anyway, this sandwich has cheese on it, too. And you definitely don't want to eat cheese. It'd be like doing two wrong things."

Steven frowned. Why did everybody insist on remembering every fact he'd told them? "One bite isn't going to kill me," he said.

"No, but if you have one bite, you might just lose all of your resolve and that wouldn't be good." Cathy shook her head.

I'm afraid it might be too late for that. I already lost my resolve, Steven thought miserably. "Just one bite," he pleaded. "And we can keep it a secret, just between you and me."

Cathy took a sip of orange juice. She hesitated, and Steven thought she must be about to give in. She started to put the sandwich right under his nose. Steven felt as though he was going to faint with happiness. Suddenly she snatched it away.

"No, I don't want to be a part of it," Cathy finally said. "You're really committed to this cause. Don't blow it just because you want one bite of a chicken sandwich."

I don't want one bite! Steven felt like screaming. *I want the whole thing!*

"So how can *you* eat it!" Steven demanded at last. "You seem to remember every one of the horrible things I told you."

"Sure," Cathy said. "And I'd like to change some of those things, like the way they're cooped up. But I like chicken. I just try not to eat a lot of it, and at home we buy free-range ones. If people start to change their habits slowly, in ways they can stick to, it could make a big, big difference."

Cathy was so intelligent and rational that sometimes Steven felt like strangling her.

Well, one thing was for sure. He couldn't wait to get home. He was going to go straight to his room and throw out all of the Katybugs' compact discs.

Ten

Jessica looked at the clock. Only an hour until Lila's party. Only sixty minutes until her life was over. Not from an earthquake, either. From total embarrassment.

She had to think of some way to keep the party from occurring. Maybe she could flood Lila's basement—that would be enough to cancel it. But then she'd probably be caught, and she'd have to pay for all the damage to the Fowler mansion.

Maybe she could shut off the electrical power. Without any lights or music, no one would want to hang around for long. Then she remembered all the flashlights Mandy had put on the tables. And Lila probably had batteries for her portable CD and tape player. Everyone would just think the darkness was part of the earthquake theme.

There had to be *something* she could do. What if she rented a bulldozer and had it go past outside the window? That would definitely make every-thing shake! Or a big trash hauler? Or just a plain old truck?

Not that she could even drive yet. She'd have to hire someone to drive. And she'd be pretty conspic-uous, driving a bulldozer on the Fowlers' lawn. Chances were good she'd get caught doing that, too.

There was only one thing to do. Jessica got on her knees and put her elbows on her bed. "I know I'm not like a model person or student or daughter or anything like that," she said, staring at the ceil-ing. "But I have to ask for a favor. I need an earth-quake to happen. Just a really little one, so no one gets hurt. It doesn't have to register on the Richter scale, or any other scale, only, there *has* to be an earthquake, or a tremor, or something. Anything. Just make the earth move. Please?"

Then Jessica remembered how they'd studied different praying rituals in social-studies class. Every country and every culture had its own way of praying. Jessica decided to do her own version of a rain dance. Sort of an earthquake dance.

She put one hand on her head and started hop-ping around her room. "Earthquake, earthquake, please come soon," she sang, hitting her bureau and desk with her hand as she danced past. "If you don't come, I'll . . ." She kept dancing until she could think of something that rhymed. "Earthquake, earthquake, please come soon. If you don't come, I'll be ruined," she chanted.

"Jessica, what are you doing?" Elizabeth stood in the doorway, laughing.

Jessica froze and she felt her cheeks get hot. "I didn't think anyone else was home."

"Are you practicing dance moves for tonight?" Elizabeth asked.

Jessica smiled sheepishly. "I was trying to make the earthquake come," she said. "But let's face it, it's not going to." She flopped onto her bed. "This night is going to be a total disaster."

"You never know," Elizabeth said. "It might work out."

"Aaron probably won't even want to go to the Valentine's dance with me, after this," Jessica whined. "Everyone's going to laugh at me."

"No, they won't," Elizabeth said.

Jessica shook her head. "Yes, they will. Elizabeth, you have to do me a favor. *Please* don't write that article about the earthquake."

"Why not? That doesn't have anything to do with your prediction," Elizabeth said.

"It doesn't?" Jessica couldn't help feeling disappointed. "Why not?"

"Because it's going to be based on fact," Elizabeth told her. "It's not about Lila's party. I mean, we might get some pictures there, but that's it."

"Are you sure?" Jessica asked.

Elizabeth nodded. "I won't mention you once. Anyway, Mr. Bowman doesn't even want us to do the article unless the earthquake comes. But who knows what'll happen? I've studied a lot about earthquakes. You might turn out to be right."

"Really? You think so?" Jessica sat up, excited.

"Yeah, you might get lucky, like last time," Elizabeth said.

"That wasn't luck—" Jessica began, but when she saw the look on Elizabeth's face, she stopped arguing. "Well, OK, maybe." Jessica crossed her fingers. "Think lucky, then," she said. "Hey, Elizabeth, do you still have that old rabbit's foot?"

"That is the coolest thing I have ever seen," Mandy said. "How does it work?"

Lila turned on the punch bowl her father had bought especially for the party that night. It had two levels. "The top bowl has a crack in it, like an earthquake hit it," Lila explained. "So the punch falls through to the bottom level, where you can get some to drink. Then these two tubes take what's in the bottom and put it back in the top, and it drips down again."

"That's great," Ellen said. "I wish I had one."

"Well, it was really expensive. But you know how Daddy is. He likes me to have the best parties," Lila said.

"This one's going to be awesome," Janet said.

"I'm glad the earthquake didn't happen while we were at school," Ellen added.

Janet let out a long, impatient sigh. "Ellen, there isn't going to *be* any earthquake." She straightened her miniskirt. "Jessica doesn't know what she's talking about. Haven't you figured that out yet?"

Mandy shrugged. "You never know. I mean, an earthquake *could* happen tonight. It's not *impossible*."

Lila rolled her eyes. "Mandy, get a life. Until Monday there hadn't been an earthquake for *twenty* years. What are the chances of two in one week?"

"Well, I believe Jessica," Ellen insisted. "She knows how it feels before an earthquake comes."

"Yeah. Only, tonight she's not going to feel anything except humiliation," Janet whispered to Lila.

Elizabeth knocked on the Suttons' front door.

"Oh, hi," Amy said, answering it a few seconds later.

"Hi," Elizabeth said. They'd barely spoken since that morning's argument. "Are you ready?"

"Yeah. Let me grab my notebook." Amy came out carrying a small notebook, and a jacket over her arm.

They walked to the car in silence. Elizabeth was

beginning to wonder whether they might be better off writing their article separately. Amy slid into the backseat on one side of Jessica, and Elizabeth slid in on the other. Mr. Wakefield was driving.

"I feel like a chauffeur, with all of you in the backseat like that," he said.

"To the Fowler mansion, please, Jeeves," Amy joked. "And step on it."

"Yes, ma'am," Mr. Wakefield said, glancing in the rearview mirror.

Elizabeth giggled. "Where's our TV? Isn't there supposed to be a TV back here?"

"And a phone," Amy said.

Elizabeth looked at Jessica. She wasn't smiling.

"Relax," Elizabeth said. "It'll be fun, earthquake or no earthquake."

"Yeah," Amy said. "And no matter what Mr. Bowman says, we should still write our article, Elizabeth. We can interview people tonight and take pictures of that cake Janet's been bragging about."

"Uh-oh—did you remember your camera?" Elizabeth asked. "I forgot mine."

Amy patted her jacket pocket. "Right here."

Elizabeth heaved a sigh of relief. "Good. And, uh, Amy? I'm sorry I yelled at you today about sleeping too much."

"That's OK," Amy said. "I should have stayed up with you."

"No, you shouldn't. Because then we'd both be so tired, we both would have forgotten our cameras," Elizabeth reasoned. "This way there's only one space cadet."

"And one total loser." Jessica sank down lower in the seat. "Will you tell everyone I was too sick to come?"

"Hello, Jessica," Lloyd said, hurrying to meet her at the Fowlers' front door. "I've been waiting for you. I'm so glad you're here early."

That makes one of us. Jessica thought she'd been so rude to Lloyd earlier that day that he wouldn't even be talking to her anymore, much less following her and hanging on her every scientific word. He sure didn't take a hint.

"How many people are here?" Jessica asked him, reluctantly following him down the stairs to the basement.

But Jessica didn't even hear his response. She saw for herself just how crowded the party was. She couldn't believe it. There were about seventy people there already, and the party had officially started only two minutes ago!

Several Unicorns were standing in a group by the cracked punch bowl. The punch was purple, of course—the official Unicorn club color.

"Excuse me." Someone pushed past Jessica to get

downstairs. As Jessica stood there at the bottom of the stairs, stunned, several more people went past on their way into the party. *The whole school's practically here!* she realized.

"Just think—you'll be able to tell everyone when to take shelter," Lloyd said. "You should be on TV tonight. You could be a local hero."

"Excuse me," Jessica said. "I think I see Mary. I need to talk to her."

"I'll come with you," Lloyd said.

Why am I not surprised? Jessica walked over to where Mary, Lila, and Ellen were standing.

"Hi, Jessica. Ready for the big night?" Ellen asked, smiling.

Jessica wanted to hit her. "Yeah, I'm ready," she said.

"Good," Lila said. "Lloyd, it's *so* nice to see you. You and Jessica are practically inseparable these days."

Jessica shot her a withering glance.

"Can you believe how many people showed up?" Lila continued. "At this rate, every single person we invited is going to come."

"Well, we *are* popular," Ellen said.

I was popular, Jessica thought miserably, looking over to where Aaron was standing.

"Listen, I'm going to go talk to Aaron," Jessica said. She wanted to get away from Lila as quickly as she could.

As she approached Aaron, she saw that he and Todd had set up a table with a sign. GUESS WHAT TIME THE EARTHQUAKE WILL HIT AND WIN A PRIZE! the sign read.

"What is this?" Jessica asked.

"Want to guess a time?" Aaron asked her. "If anyone would know, it's you."

"Um, I don't think so," Jessica said.

"Whoever guesses closest to the time of the quake without going over gets a ten-dollar gift certificate to Casey's. Lila's dad sprang for it," Todd explained.

"Come on, Jessica. Give it a try," Aaron urged her.

"Uh . . . thanks, but I need to tell Elizabeth something," Jessica said. "See ya."

"Lloyd, what about you?" she heard Aaron ask as she disappeared into the crowd.

Jessica collapsed on a couch in the corner of the basement. She was cranky and exhausted after having slept so badly the night before. *I just want to hide. I wish I were invisible,* she thought. She couldn't believe Aaron was taking bets on when the earthquake would happen! Did he have to humiliate her even more?

Jessica was still on the couch, yawning as she listened to Lloyd blab about tectonic plates and graph patterns. Suddenly she saw Lila headed over to them. *Now what*, she thought.

"So, are you two having fun?" Lila smiled at Jessica and Lloyd.

"I'll be getting some punch now," Lloyd said. "Would anyone else care for some?"

Jessica shook her head. "No, thanks."

"Good idea. You wouldn't want to be drinking punch when the earthquake comes," Lila said. "It would spill all over your new white shirt."

Jessica drummed her fingers on the arm of the couch. If that's how Lila was going to be, there was only one thing to do. Act just as confident as she had been. She wasn't going to give in until she had to. "I'm not worried about my shirt," she said smoothly.

"Anyway, I guess you don't think—I mean, feel—that this one's going to be very strong after all, or you wouldn't have come," Lila said. "You know, with the danger and everything you warned everyone about."

Jessica shrugged. "Well, you know. As long as everyone else was going to be here, it wouldn't look right for the guest of honor not to show up." She smiled at Lila. *Take that!*

"So . . . I shouldn't worry about damage to our house?" Lila asked.

"No, I think this one will be very mild—even milder than the last one," Jessica said. "Which, if you recall, I did experience firsthand," she added smugly.

One of Lila's eyebrows arched. She did not look amused. "Did you make your bet on what time it'll hit?"

"No," Jessica said. "You see, with the way the plates underneath Sweet Valley are, it's very difficult to say exactly when—"

"Forget the Lloyd act," Lila said. "It's not working. If you're such an expert, come over to the booth with me and make your bet. It should be a sure ten bucks," Lila said, flashing her a phony smile. "Unless you've been *lying* this entire time."

Jessica got up and went over to the table. Who cared if she guessed wrong? She was too sick of listening to Lila to sit there for another minute.

"Ready to make a guess?" Todd asked her.

"I think so." Jessica furrowed her brow in concentration. "Ah . . . let me see. I'm going to say . . . Hmm." Jessica tapped her finger on her chin. "Maybe . . . but no."

"Just get it over with!" Lila demanded.

Jessica glared at her. "You can't rush a genius."

"How would *you* know," Lila muttered. She and Jessica stared at each other angrily.

Jessica turned to Todd. "I say the earthquake is going to occur sometime in the next hour." She glanced at her watch. "It's seven thirty now. It'll happen by eight thirty."

"Can't you be more precise than *that*?" Lila sneered. "We all picked exact times."

"And you all don't know half as much as I do about this," Jessica said defiantly. "These things are very difficult to pin down."

Lila looked as if she was about to explode.

"Hey, everybody!" Todd called, as Aaron ran over to turn down the CD player. "Jessica predicts that the earthquake will occur within the next hour! Keep your eyes and ears open!"

And your mouth shut, Jessica wanted to tell Todd, frowning at him.

"All right, Jessica!" a couple of people shouted.

"Get ready for the quake!" someone added.

"And don't forget to buy your official T-shirt!" Bruce yelled.

It seemed as if everyone really was expecting an earthquake. Everyone except Jessica.

Eleven

"Did you hear that?" Elizabeth asked Amy. "If Jessica's right, we'll have to stay awake for only another hour."

"Don't tell me *you* believe her now," Amy said.

Elizabeth yawned. "Right now I'd believe anything, if it meant I could go to sleep earlier." She was sitting in a large, comfortable chair, and she was curled up into a little ball. She had almost fallen asleep twice.

"How can you be so sleepy? Look at everyone dancing." Amy pointed at the cluster of people dancing to one of Lila's many new CDs.

"I couldn't dance if my life depended on it," Elizabeth said.

She watched as Amy got up and circled the party, taking photographs of everyone. She really did wish

Jessica's prediction turned out to be right. Not just because she'd get to go home and crawl into her very own bed and sleep for nine hours, but because no matter how stupidly her sister acted, she hated to see Lila beat her. Jessica and Lila had been rivals and best friends forever. It was fun watching them compete, but Elizabeth always rooted for Jessica—even when she knew Jessica was being ridiculous.

When Amy came back to check on Elizabeth a few minutes later, she was practically snoozing again. "I can't believe this," Amy said, panting.

"What?" Elizabeth asked.

"I just took a picture of Jessica and Lloyd, and Jessica threw a fit," Amy explained. "She's like those celebrities who hate having their picture taken. For a second I thought she was going to punch me."

Elizabeth lazily stretched her arms over her head. "Jessica loves having her picture taken. Just not with Lloyd. She probably thinks we'll put it in the *Sixers*."

Amy giggled. "That *would* be funny. On the gossip page."

"She'd kill me," Elizabeth said, grinning.

"Well, right now, I think the first person on her hit list is Lloyd," Amy said. "You should have heard him. He's following her around like a dog."

"Well, if her prediction doesn't pan out, at least she'll have one thing to be happy about: no more Lloyd," Elizabeth said.

"What's fascinating is that the plates underneath the earth move an average of three-thousandths of an inch a day," Lloyd said. "The rock layers usually catch hold of each other. But sometimes the pressure is too much."

"No kidding," Jessica mumbled, feeling her eyelids grow heavy.

"And then the plate jumps forward into a new position—that's what makes an earthquake happen. Of course, that's just the most basic explanation. It doesn't begin to cover the magical terror of earthquakes."

Jessica yawned. She wanted to tell Lloyd he had a great future as a filmstrip narrator. He was just as knowledgeable—and just as boring.

Jessica couldn't sit still and listen to Lloyd go on any longer. Already fifteen minutes of her hour had passed, and nothing had happened. Not that she was surprised.

She got up and walked over to the table where Bruce was selling his T-shirts.

"Seven forty-five," Bruce greeted her, pointing at his expensive gold watch.

"I know," Jessica said in an irritated voice. Did he think she couldn't tell time?

"I've sold twenty-five T-shirts so far," he told her.

"That's great!" she said.

Bruce shook his head. "Not when I had a hundred printed up, it isn't." He held one up for Jessica. "What do you say? Large or extra large?"

"I don't have enough money," Jessica said. Bruce was selling the T-shirts for ten dollars each. "But maybe I can convince Elizabeth to get one."

"Well, all I can say is, if this earthquake doesn't happen tonight, *nobody's* going to want these shirts. They have today's date on them, you know. I'll probably have to give everyone their money back, too." Bruce frowned at Jessica.

"It's not my fault you made too many," Jessica said. "Anyway, there's still lots of time."

Bruce's eyes narrowed suspiciously. "Look, Jessica. You have forty-five more minutes. If the earthquake doesn't happen by then, you're going to owe me for a hundred T-shirts. At five dollars each, that comes to . . ."

"It's coming, it's coming!" Jessica insisted, edging away from the table. "Just chill out already."

Not only was she going to be humiliated, she was going to owe Bruce Patman five hundred dollars? Jessica went to the bathroom and locked the door. Then, very quietly, she started to do the earthquake dance again.

"Hey, Jessica. Want to know the running total?" Aaron asked as she walked past his table ten minutes later.

"Total what?" Jessica asked warily.

"We started taking new bets, just for fun," Aaron told her. "The new bet is how many people think *your* time prediction is going to come true."

Jessica groaned. "Great. Go ahead, give me the bad news."

"OK. Well, seventy-seven people think you're wrong. And, uh . . ." He consulted a sheet of paper on the table. "One person thinks you're right."

"Lloyd," Jessica said, rolling her eyes.

"You could make it seventy-seven to two," Aaron offered.

"It doesn't matter," Jessica said. She was feeling so hopeless, she wouldn't even bet on herself.

"It's eight o'clock," Aaron said cheerfully. "Only half an hour to go!"

Only half an hour until doomsday, Jessica thought, walking over to Mandy, Mary, and Grace. "Are *you* guys having fun?" she asked the group.

"Definitely," Grace said. "How about you?"

Jessica shrugged. She'd rather be taking a science quiz, but she wasn't going to admit that to any of the Unicorns. "It's OK. Where's that cake Janet kept talking about?"

"I think she's saving it for the . . . uh . . . climax," Mary said. "You know, when the earthquake comes."

"I wish she'd bring it out now," Mandy said, rubbing her stomach. "I'm hungry."

"She might be waiting a long time," Jessica muttered under her breath. *Like a couple of hundred years.*

Steven had been standing at the top of the stairs for almost fifteen minutes, waiting for his parents to go into the den or the living room so he could sneak into the kitchen and grab a bowl of ice cream, some cheese and crackers, a ham sandwich—anything! But they were just sitting at the kitchen table, like they had been ever since dinner, yakking about nothing.

Finally he heard a chair move. He listened to his mother's voice trail off as she moved into the living room, and his father followed her.

Steven waited another minute, then tiptoed down the stairs. He could grab a box of Baco-Cheez crackers and be back upstairs in five seconds. If they were watching television, he'd have more options, but he didn't want to risk getting caught.

Steven pulled open the cabinet door. It creaked a little, but he did it quickly. He had his hand on the box of crackers when he heard his father clear his throat. "Having some rice cakes?" Mr. Wakefield asked.

Steven unclenched the box of crackers and grabbed the end of a package of rice cakes. "Yeah. They were just kind of wedged in the back here," he said sheepishly. He undid the twist-tie and held out

the rice cakes to his father. "Want some?"

"A rice cake sounds like a good idea," Mr. Wakefield said. "How about some peanut butter on top?"

"Uh . . . sure," Steven said. He grimaced as he sat at the table with his father and spread all-natural peanut butter on a rice cake. He used to like rice cakes, but when he had his stomach set on Baco-Cheez crackers, they were pretty disappointing.

"Steven, you've given the house a whole new way of life," Mr. Wakefield said cheerfully, crunching into a rice cake. "I feel a hundred percent better on this no-meat diet."

That makes one of us, Steven thought.

"Jessica! It's almost eight thirty!" Lila cried, shutting off the music. Everyone on the dance floor stopped moving and looked around, as if they were expecting an earthquake any second.

Jessica chewed her thumbnail and studied her watch. *One minute until my life is over.* She watched the second hand sweep around the dial. Each second seemed to last forever.

"Five . . . four . . . three . . . two . . . one!" the crowd shouted.

They all stood waiting in silence.

Nothing happened.

"Well?" Lila said, coming over to her.

"Uh . . ." Jessica faltered as she noticed a hundred

faces, practically everyone at Sweet Valley Middle School, looking at her from all over the room. "Where's that earthcake, anyway?" she joked.

Nobody laughed.

"You said it would come in an hour, and it's been an hour," Lila reminded her.

Jessica saw Bruce giving her an angry look. "Did I say *one* hour?" she asked, trying to sound innocent. She shook her head. "I'm sorry. The vibrations I'm getting say it's going to be at least another hour. Maybe two."

Even Lloyd was looking at Jessica as if she were lying through her teeth.

"So there's really no point in sticking around, because it might be really late tonight when it happens, like last time," Jessica said quickly.

"Nobody's leaving," Lila said. "Not until we find out if there really is an earthquake coming today." She stared at Jessica. "Whatever time it is."

"Hey, I didn't say I was giving up," Jessica said. "I'm staying until it happens. But if I was off by a few hours, it could be three in the morning again." Jessica heard a little grumbling in the crowd. She hoped people were deciding to go home.

"We'll see," Lila said, her arms folded across her chest.

"But then, that would be tomorrow—and you'd be *wrong*."

Jessica shrugged. "It's not an exact science." She was relieved when someone turned the music back up. She got a cup of punch and went to sit in the corner by herself. *Dynamite*, she thought. *I should have exploded some dynamite outside the house.*

She would have gone to jail, but it would probably be better than having to walk into school tomorrow morning and face everyone.

Twelve

"I'm taking off," Todd told Elizabeth at nine fifteen.

"Don't you want to wait and find out if anyone won the bet?" Elizabeth asked sleepily.

"No offense," Todd said. "But this party's pretty beat. Jessica's obviously pulling our legs."

"OK, well, I'll see you tomorrow," she said weakly. She couldn't blame Todd. Everybody was feeling the same way. *Poor Jessica*, she thought, looking around the room for her sister.

Where was Jessica, anyway?

Jessica peeked around the corner. Finally! A place where Lloyd wouldn't find her. It was a nook of the basement that housed the hot-water heater, a few pairs of skis, and an old beanbag chair.

This is the worst night of my life, Jessica thought.

Maybe she should start being nicer to Lloyd, she mused. Because after tonight, he might be her only friend.

It was already nine thirty, and people were beginning to realize that the whole thing was a hoax.

Jessica sank down into the beanbag chair with a yawn. She looked up at an inflatable globe spinning on the ceiling. She wished her parents would show up early, for once, instead of at ten o'clock. She didn't know if she could stand another fifteen minutes in Lila's basement.

It's never going to happen. And I'm never going to hear the end of it.

Her eyelids grew heavy as she began to daydream about the earthquake.

"What a bust."

"I'm really getting sick of waiting."

"We should have known Jessica was full of it."

"Where is Jessica, anyway?"

Lila couldn't help smiling as she watched her guests milling around the basement. There were half-full cups of punch all over the place, and most of the rock candy was crushed into bits on the floor. A few chocolate milk shakes had spilled.

She never thought she'd actually enjoy seeing one of her parties go down the tubes. But this was working out perfectly. And it was time for the final step of her plan. Time to finish Jessica off.

Lila turned the music off and stepped into the center of the room. "OK, everybody. Shut up for a second!"

She waited until she had everyone's attention.

"Listen, I realize you're all really disappointed," Lila said to her audience, trying to look sincere. "Jessica Wakefield had convinced us all that there would be an earthquake tonight. And we were all counting on it." She heard grumbles of agreement from the crowd. "Now it's obvious that there won't be an earthquake, and that Jessica is a big phony. But before you go home, we'll serve the earthcake, and try to make the best of a *very* disappointing evening."

There was more grumbling from the group.

"Don't tell me how angry you are," Lila said, her palms to the ceiling. "Tell *Jessica*."

"Come on, let's get some pictures of Lila carrying the cake down the stairs," Amy said to Elizabeth. "I have only three left on this roll of film. I might as well use them up." She sighed. "Not that there's going to be an article in this."

Janet had dimmed the lights, and everyone was gathering around to get a good look at the cake. It was decorated with icing and little plastic houses from a Monopoly set to look like a miniature Sweet Valley.

"That's really—" Suddenly Elizabeth stopped. She looked down at her feet. She felt a slight rumbling and glanced over her shoulder to see if anyone was still dancing.

No way! she thought to herself. *There's just no way!*

But then she saw the plastic cups on the table quivering. One of them jumped off the edge of the table and fell to the floor, spilling punch in a widening purple pool.

Elizabeth started toward Amy. She felt strange, slightly off balance, and as if she were moving in slow motion.

"Omigod!" she shouted in disbelief. "It's an—"

"*Earthquake!*" at least twenty other voices screamed.

All of a sudden, the entire basement full of people burst into chaos.

But there was one bloodcurdling shriek that Elizabeth heard clearly over all the others. It was the sound of Lila tumbling headfirst into the earthcake.

Yes!

Steven opened the refrigerator and looked inside. His parents had just left to pick up Jessica and Elizabeth, and he had the whole house to himself. He'd have to hurry, because it wouldn't take them long to get back.

Steven was going to have the fastest pig-out in

history. There was just one problem. Now that the whole family had practically gone vegetarian, there was barely anything in the refrigerator he wanted to eat.

He had to take something no one would miss. He rearranged the jars on the top shelf. "Aha!" There it was. A jar of leftover homemade spaghetti sauce—made with his dad's famous sausage meatballs. He could put some on an English muffin—make that a slice of whole wheat and sunflower-seed bread—and melt some cheese on top of it, for a mini-pizza.

Do you really want to do that? Cathy's words echoed in his head.

Steven hesitated. He did believe in vegetarianism. He knew that eating less meat was a good idea. He'd be healthier. If the whole family stopped eating meat, they'd be helping the planet in more ways than one.

But, on the other hand, was one little snack going to make a difference? Steven didn't think so.

He grabbed the jar and turned around. He was halfway to the counter when he heard a strange rattling sound. He spun around to face the sink and realized all the glass canisters were shaking. He leaped in surprise when he heard his mother's framed picture of wildflowers crash to the floor.

"Earthquake!" Steven cried. He was so startled, he dropped the jar of spaghetti sauce.

It exploded on the floor, glass shattering, tomato sauce spreading in a flood of red. A meatball bounced underneath the refrigerator.

"Arrrrgh!" Steven cried.

He looked around the room in desperation as the rattling finally stopped. He had a huge mess on his hands. And if he didn't clean it up by the time his parents came home, everyone would know exactly what he had been up to.

Steven grabbed a roll of paper towels and got on his hands and knees. But all the paper towels did was smear the sauce around. For a second Steven was afraid it was actually staining the Spanish tiles redder.

He went to the utility closet and got out the mop and bucket. He hurriedly filled the bucket with hot water and cleaning solution, sloshing it all over the floor.

"Couldn't the stupid earthquake have waited until I was done eating?" he shouted at the refrigerator.

There was so much screaming and rushing around that it was hard to tell when the earthquake actually stopped. When Elizabeth finally decided that it had, the room exploded again. Everybody started laughing, and hugging, and giving each other high-fives.

"We made it!"

"It was totally awesome!"

"It really happened!"

"I can't believe it! Jessica was right!"

At the bottom of the stairs, Elizabeth saw Lila extricating herself from the earthcake with as much dignity as possible. When Lila finally got to her feet, everyone started laughing even harder. She had green frosting all over one side of her face and stuck in big clumps in her hair.

"I have to get a picture of this," Amy said, laughing as she rushed over. Elizabeth saw the flash of the bulb and heard Lila's angry squeal.

She shook her head, unable to suppress a giggle. Jessica, the single luckiest human being on the face of the earth, had gone from being an outcast to a star. And Lila was covered with bright-green icing and little red Monopoly hotels. "It ain't over till it's over," she muttered to herself.

Jessica must be getting a huge kick out of this, she thought, looking around the room.

Where was Jessica, anyway?

"Where is Jessica?" Amy asked. She had a big smile on her face, and her camera in her hand. "I have one last shot, and I want to get a picture of the amazing, incredible, extrasensory Madame Wakefield."

"Can you believe she got away with this?" Elizabeth asked.

"Got away with it?" Amy laughed. "I'm beginning to think Jessica really does have special powers. And so does everybody else."

Elizabeth shook her head. "I'm sure she's off gloating somewhere. She'll be bragging about this for weeks." Elizabeth smiled. "Come on, let's go find her."

Elizabeth was surprised that her sister wasn't in the middle of the floor, basking in her glory. Jessica wasn't with the other Unicorns, she wasn't tormenting Lila, she wasn't by the stereo, or even in the bathroom. *Where was she?*

Elizabeth felt a twinge of worry. Jessica couldn't have been hurt in the earthquake, could she? Elizabeth didn't think it had been strong enough, but still . . . "Amy, you don't think . . ." Elizabeth began slowly.

Suddenly she stopped.

In a small nook in the basement, between what appeared to be a hot-water heater and a pair of skis, a shoe was sticking out. A very familiar shoe. She tugged on Amy's sleeve. "Look."

Amy's eyes widened, and they crept over.

There was Jessica, curled up on the floor, sound asleep.

"I don't believe it," Elizabeth said, laughing.

"Shh," Amy whispered. "Don't wake her up yet." Amy focused the camera and snapped a picture.

The flash went off, and Jessica jerked awake. "What happened?" she asked, looking up at them and rubbing her eyes. "What are you guys laughing at?"

"What a night. What an incredible night," Jessica said, rummaging around in the Wakefields' refrigerator after Lila's party. She had been so nervous at the party she hadn't eaten a thing, and now she was starving. "Can you believe it, Lizzie? Am I amazing or what?" she asked, poking her head out of the refrigerator for a moment.

"Amazing," Elizabeth said wryly, collapsing into a chair at the kitchen table.

"Cool! There's a little mint-chocolate-chip ice cream left. I was worried I was going to be stuck with rice cakes and that foul-tasting peanut butter," Jessica said, plunking the carton of ice cream down on the counter.

"It's probably a good thing you're finishing it off," Elizabeth said, "so it won't be around to tempt Steven."

Jessica shook her head. "I have a feeling Steven may be a lost cause."

"Really? What makes you say that?" Elizabeth asked.

"Because the other morning I almost caught him using real milk," Jessica said. "Dad surprised him and he quickly switched to soy milk."

"You're kidding," Elizabeth said. She opened the trash can to put in the empty ice-cream carton. "Wow! Maybe you're not kidding. Look at this."

"Elizabeth, I don't want to look at the trash," Jessica protested.

"Just look," Elizabeth urged her. Jessica got up and went over to the garbage can. Elizabeth pointed to a broken jar. "See that?" She pointed to some meatballs in the trash. "And those?"

"Gross," Jessica commented.

"We didn't eat that for dinner," Elizabeth reminded her. "That's the jar that had leftover meatball spaghetti sauce in it. And Steven *was* home by himself."

"So you think he ate it? But why would it be all smashed up and in the trash?" Jessica asked. "It doesn't make any sense."

Elizabeth snapped her fingers. "The earthquake! I bet it had something to do with the earthquake," she said with a grin. "Look." She pointed to a meatball that was poking out from underneath the refrigerator.

Jessica burst out laughing. "He must have dropped the jar!"

Elizabeth started laughing too. "I have a feeling Steven is cracking."

"I'm sure of it," Jessica said, a scheming sparkle in her eye. "And I have a perfect plan to catch him in the act."

Thirteen

"Elizabeth, how could you do this to me?" Jessica shoved the newest edition of the *Sixers* in front of Elizabeth's face in social-studies class Friday afternoon.

Right on the front page was a picture of Jessica, sound asleep on the floor at Lila's party. The caption read, "SECOND SWEET VALLEY EARTHQUAKE IS A REAL SNOOZE!"

Elizabeth smiled. "Pretty good, huh?"

"It's not funny! How did you even get this in here so fast, anyway?" Jessica demanded.

"Amy dropped her film off at one of those one-hour developing places this morning. We had the rest of the issue ready to go," Elizabeth explained.

"Couldn't you have used some *other* picture?" Jessica asked. "Look at me. I have dust in my hair, and my mouth is wide open." Jessica glanced at the photo again and shuddered. Was that drool on her shirt? She hoped she didn't really look like that.

"Did you look inside yet?" Elizabeth asked.

"No," Jessica grumbled.

"Well, take a look." Elizabeth handed the paper back to her.

Jessica opened it to the second page and burst out laughing. "That's great! Ooooh. Look at all that frosting on her face!"

It was the picture of Lila climbing out of the cake. Lila had a startled look on her face—and she was so angry, her eyes were almost crossed.

"Couldn't you have put *her* on the front page?" Jessica demanded.

"I credited you with guessing when the earthquake would come," Elizabeth said. "Isn't that good enough?"

Just then Aaron came into class, carrying a copy of the *Sixers*. "Hey, nice picture, Jessica!" he called to her from the front of the classroom.

Winston started laughing. "Jessica can predict them—she just can't stay awake for them!" he added.

"Special scientific powers, huh, Jess?" Mandy said, coming into the room with the newspaper in her hand.

"How could you sleep through an earthquake you predicted?" Mary asked with a giggle.

Jessica just shrugged. Her face was pink, but she was smiling. "I'm calm under pressure. What can I say?"

"There he is." Elizabeth pointed toward the front door of Sweet Valley High School. "And he's alone."

"So?" Jessica asked.

"So there's probably a reason he's alone," Elizabeth said.

"Yeah, he's been acting like a real jerk to everyone," Jessica said.

"Not that," Elizabeth said. "I mean, because he wants to sneak off and buy some food he's not supposed to."

The twins watched as Steven unlocked his bicycle. Then, pedaling quickly, they started off behind him. "Make sure he doesn't see you," Elizabeth warned Jessica.

"I'm not stupid," Jessica said. "I know how to follow someone."

"Taking lessons from Lloyd?" Elizabeth teased.

"Ha ha," Jessica said, riding behind her. "I'll have you know this is the first day all week I haven't had to eat lunch with him. I really missed him, too."

Elizabeth turned around and looked at her.

"Gotcha," Jessica said with a smile. "Look out for that bump."

Elizabeth's bicycle bounced on the road, and she

turned back around and concentrated on following Steven. "I think he's heading toward the beach," she said a few minutes later.

All of a sudden Steven turned around. Jessica and Elizabeth swerved into an alley. "Phew," Jessica said. "That was close." She peeked out into the street. "OK, we can go now."

"You know what's at the beach," Elizabeth said, shifting into higher gear.

"Annie's Avocado Heaven," said Jessica.

"Strictly Sprouts," Elizabeth added.

"Hughie's Burger Shack!" they both yelled at the same time.

Steven stepped up to the counter. The moment he'd been dreaming of was finally here. He was about to enter heaven.

"Can I help you?" a boy wearing a Hughie's hat asked him.

"Yeah. Uh . . ." Steven wasn't sure where to begin. "Give me a minute." His big moment, and he couldn't decide what to order. He wanted everything. "OK," he told the boy after another minute. "I'd like the big burger basket. And an extra-thick chocolate shake."

"Small or large?"

"Large." Steven felt a twinge of guilt, remembering what he had learned about meat and dairy products. But when the boy slid his order across the counter, and the smell of the hamburger reached his nose, everything vanished from his mind. He sat at the first empty table he could find.

He was halfway through the double hamburger, savoring every bite, when he saw something that made the food in his mouth turn to sawdust.

Jessica and Elizabeth walked into the restaurant.

"Hi, Steven. How's your burger?" Jessica asked. "Mm . . . looks good."

Steven started choking on his burger. "I—I wasn't eating this," he said, trying to catch his breath and swallow as quickly as possible. He shoved the tray away. "I mean . . . someone just left this here. I'm waiting for my . . . onion rings." He smiled nervously. "Raw onions. Not fried."

"Is it OK if we sit with you?" Elizabeth asked, pulling out a chair.

"Sure." Steven glanced at his hamburger. He was dying to keep eating. "So aren't you guys going to order anything?" Maybe if they went up to the counter, he'd have time to finish the burger and stuff the wrapper into the trash.

"You know, I'd really like to," Jessica said. "But there's just nothing on the menu I can eat."

"Yeah, it's really terrible, isn't it? All that meat." Elizabeth picked the bun off the burger and poked at it. "Who knows how many pesticides are in there."

Steven scuffed the floor with his high-top sneaker. "Yeah, I know," he said weakly.

"Well, even if the burger's OK, what about the cheese? Not to mention the ketchup," Jessica said, shaking her head. "Ketchup is full of sugar, and we know how awful *that* is."

"Can you believe anyone would eat mustard?" Elizabeth said. "They must be crazy. They must not care about all those poor mustard-seed plants."

"And pickles!" Jessica exclaimed, picking one up and making a face at it. "Dis-gusting."

"Not to mention—"

"OK, OK!" Steven cried. "I get it already! I'm a jerk. I'm a loser." He looked up sheepishly. "Jess, could you pass me my burger?"

Elizabeth and Jessica burst into laughter.

"Steven, even though you've been a big pain in the neck about it," Elizabeth began, "this vegetarian thing wasn't a bad idea."

"Actually, some of it was pretty good," Jessica added.

"It's definitely better for the planet," Elizabeth said. "It was just that you were telling us what not to eat all the time—"

"And ruining our appetites," Jessica cut in.

"I know." Steven sighed. "I mean, I really am going to try to eat a lot less meat. And I already wrote some letters to protest the way animals are treated. But I can't give up everything."

"Before we give you your burger back, you have to promise us one thing," Elizabeth said as Steven grabbed his quickly melting milk shake.

"Anything." Steven stirred it with a straw.

"Whatever you eat in the future, whether it's burgers, tofu, or sunflowers, just don't make everyone else eat it too."

"Deal," Steven said.

"You know what? I think I'll get something after all," Elizabeth said.

"Me too," Jessica said. "I'm hungry."

The twins came back to the table a few minutes later, just as Steven was finishing his hamburger. "What did you get?" he asked, staring at a strange-looking burger on Elizabeth's plate.

"It's a tempeh burger," Elizabeth said. "Want to try it?"

"Uh . . . what's it made out of?" Steven asked.

"Soybeans, mostly." Elizabeth took a big bite. "Sure you don't want some?"

"No, thanks." Steven was about to make a face. Then he stopped himself. "But you go right ahead. It looks delicious."

"Those pictures of you guys in the *Sixers* were so hilarious," Ellen said on Monday morning in the lunchroom. "Everybody was talking about them in gym class this morning."

Lila frowned at her. "It's old news. The paper came out last week. Doesn't anyone around here have anything better to talk about?" she grumbled.

"I do," Mandy said excitedly, setting her tray down on the table. "Children's Hospital is starting a big charity drive, and I thought of a great way to raise money."

"So what is it?" Jessica asked.

Mandy had had cancer earlier that year and had been treated at Children's Hospital. She was healthy now, but Jessica knew how important the hospital was to Mandy.

"Have you guys ever heard of those auctions where people bid for other people's time?" Mandy asked. "The bidders pay a certain amount to go out on a date with someone, or have a meal cooked for them, or whatever."

"Yeah, I've seen those!" Jessica said excitedly. "They have an auction like that every year at Sweet Valley High. It's only for the seniors. Anyone can buy them for the day—and use them as their personal servants."

"Exactly!" Mandy said. "We'll do the same thing, only we'll be the ones for sale."

"You mean . . . the Unicorns?" Lila asked.

Mandy nodded. "Yeah. And we'll donate all the

money we make to the hospital. I bet we can raise a lot."

Jessica looked at Lila and grinned. Lila? A servant for a day? This was going to be awesome!

What will happen when the Unicorns donate themselves for charity? Find out in Sweet Valley Twins and Friends #76, **YOURS FOR A DAY.**